Morri

The 7th Ron

Pete

Gruff Books © 2024

We are like books. Most people only see our cover, the minority read only the introduction, many people believe the critics. Few will know our content.

Emile Zola

This book is dedicated to Mike Garland and his son Adam, both of East Suffolk Morris, plus his daughter Emma Melville of Anker Morris. All three have become Squires to the Morris Ring and have done much to develop Morris dancing in Suffolk and the UK.

The Ron Webb Mystery Series:

Dog Walk Detectives	(2021) #1
Conveyor Belt Corpse	(2021) #2
Surreptitious Cyclist	(2021) #3
An Angry Arsonist	(2022) #4
Murder amongst the Mounds	(2023) #5
Holistic Homicide	(2024) #6
Morris Murder	(2024) #7

All were published by Gruff Books.

All events and characters in this book are fictional and do not represent other events or people, living or dead, past or present.

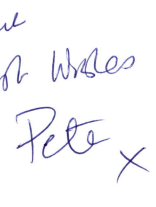

Morris Murder

Chapter 1

Thursday 9th March, 2017

23-year-old Archie Berry shouted goodnight to his mate in Woolpit Village Hall carpark at about 10 pm and got into his red Ford Fiesta, throwing his empty water bottle onto the passenger seat and giving a little shiver in the night air. After building up a light sweat at the morris dance practice, he had put on a sweatshirt and turned the car's heater on as he pulled away. The clouds hid the moon, so it was dark once Archie left the village. Some lively folk tunes by *Bellowhead* issued loudly from his stereo as he headed out on the Elmswell road en route to his home in Walsham-le-Willows, Suffolk.

He never arrived. He carried straight across the road at full speed on a left-hand bend and took off on a low verge before launching into an oak tree in an apparent attempt to climb it. The engine was rammed back through the bulwark into his chest, killing him instantly amidst a sickening crunch. The tattered white fragments of the airbag were no defence against such a powerful force. Debris of glass, plastic and metal came raining down into the front seats. Grass and mud from the verge hung off the wheel arches and chassis. There was a smell of petrol and oil leaking from the mangled vehicle, and the car bonnet, like a swimmer, appeared bent into a pike position as part of its dive into oblivion. Muddy ruts trailed the car across the grassy verge from the road. Somehow, the headlights continued functioning, pointing up at the tree from the now corrugated bonnet with beams that lit its bare winter branches. Five minutes later, those lights alerted another motorist to the crash, who got onto his mobile phone in a shaky voice to report it.

The paramedics could do nothing except confirm that the man was dead until the fire service harshly lit up the scene with a portable arc light and cut through metal and the seat belt to release his lifeless, bloodied corpse. They transferred it straight onto the stretcher for the ambulance. A traffic policeman parked his car up the road with lights flashing and road signs in both directions to alert any other motorists of the accident. He spoke on his radio to summon a tow truck and advise his colleagues back at base that he would likely remain there until it arrived. He had to pause for the noise of the fire engine winch pulling the vehicle from the tree, leaving white scars where the bark had been ripped off the trunk. PC Richards had put the registration number into the system, which gave him a probable identity. It was confirmed by removing the wallet from the body, which held Archibald Berry's driving licence.

After walking up the road to make observations, Richards took photographs and measurements with a colleague who had joined him. Dave swept some odd debris off the edge of the road where the car had mounted the verge and, with the wreck eventually loaded onto the back of a truck, got back into his vehicle to carry out the worst part of the job of all.

By midnight, PC Dave Richards was knocking on the door of a semi-detached house in Walsham-le-Willows. The house was initially dark, but a light appeared in a front bedroom window, and the curtain moved. Expecting that his son had once again forgotten his key, the occupant was startled to see a police car outside instead. He hurriedly put on a dressing gown and let the officer in.

"Are you the father of Archibald Berry?" Dave asked as soon as he was invited inside.

Mr Berry Senior nodded with a frightened look on his face. "What has happened? He was at morris practice tonight. I thought he was late back when we went to bed but guessed maybe he had stopped for a drink with his friends."

"I regret to tell you that he had a crash outside Woolpit tonight. I'm sad to say that he did not survive, so I am very sorry for your loss," pronounced the officer gravely.

A cry went up from the doorway to the lounge. Mrs Berry had come down to see what was happening and had overheard the conversation. "Not my Archie!" she wailed. "My darling boy. No, it can't be true!" She dissolved into heaving sobs whilst her husband stoically put his arm around her shoulder, unsure of what else to do. He stared into the middle distance, trying to make sense of what he was being told. There was some further talk about identifying the body and other practicalities before the policeman left them to their misery.

Chapter 2

Friday, 10th March, 2017

The Suffolk Serious Crime Squad room was relatively quiet this afternoon. DCI Ron Webb was upstairs with 'His Lordship', and the rest of the team endeavoured to finish their collective paperwork from the latest case. Since between them, they had arrested twelve suspects yesterday in a significant cigarette smuggling operation at Felixstowe Docks and elsewhere, they had a lot to do, with fingers tapping at keyboards and furrowed brows the order of the day. Occasionally, someone would consult a pocketbook and try to decipher what crucial note they had scribbled in a dark, wet docklands with little time to spare. The operation, with a number of covert stake-out observations over several weeks in conjunction with HM Customs and Excise, had been complicated. Still, they got a good result and caught the kingpins. They were disturbed by a sharp knock on the door and the entry of a uniformed traffic officer. It was PC Dave Richards.

Grey-suited DS Peggy Catchpole looked up from her screen sharply, almost sensing the presence of Dave Richards before seeing him. It was a shock for her since they were currently going through a divorce, and she hadn't seen him since he removed his belongings from their old home. (She retained her maiden name at work when she married.)

"Good morning. How are you?" Richards asked hesitatingly.

"Alright," she replied coldly. "What do you want?"

"I have a case we need to transfer. Is your boss about?"

"He is upstairs now but should soon be back," Catchpole replied. "You'd better come and wait in his office." Usually, she would have offered a cup of tea to a visitor, but she saw no reason to be nice to her cheating ex-husband. He followed her through to the office and sat down.

"Have you settled into your new flat, ok?" Dave asked, trying to find something polite to say to break their awkward silence.

"Yes, it's fine and conveniently close to here," Peggy volunteered. "Ah, here comes DCI Webb", she added, relieved as she spotted her boss entering the squad room. He wore a dark suit, white shirt, tie, and dazzlingly polished shoes. He was in his fifties, with a broad face and piercing eyes. He was known as a successful and 'safe pair of hands' with which to handle the high-profile cases that came his way. Relieved by the interruption, Peggy exited the room and told Ron he had a visitor. He glanced through the open door.

"That's your ex, isn't it?" he asked kindly. She nodded. "Are you OK?"

"Fine, thank you, sir," she replied. Always aware that a woman replying 'fine' could mean anything but, Ron joined his guest and closed the door. Peggy returned to her seat at the computer, aware that DC Will Cateby, sitting on the opposite side of the desk, probably recognised Dave from social occasions as well. He wisely kept his head down and avoided eye contact. He wore a blue shirt, habitually open at the neck unless he went out and the sleeves rolled up. He was not confident with women but knew better than to comment about Dave's visit to his Sergeant.

Inside Ron's inner sanctum, Richards was beginning to explain the reason for his visit. "I attended an RTA[1] last night outside Woolpit. A young man called Archie Berry had piled his car into a tree and died. It was on a left-hand bend, but he appeared to have continued straight across the road, mounted the grass verge and hit the tree with enough impact to push the car a little way up the trunk. Initially, one thinks about a young man driving too fast and losing control, but there didn't appear to be any skid marks from braking."

---

[1] RTA Road Traffic Accident

"Could he have collapsed at the wheel beforehand, PC Richards?" asked Ron.

"I don't think so. I saw his body before the Fire Brigade cut it out. His arms were crossed against his head, and his body was tilted towards the offside as if to avoid the impact."

"So you think he knew what was happening then?" queried Webb.

"Yes, and as far as we know, drugs and drink were not involved. It's possible that he might have been avoiding an animal, such as a deer, on the road, but it couldn't have been caused by getting dazzled. It was a left-hand bend for him, so someone driving from the opposite direction shouldn't have caused any problems. He had just been attending a practice of a morris dance group in Woolpit, according to his father. He crashed just after 10 pm, so it doesn't appear he had stopped off at a pub afterwards, although we do not know. It was enough for me to be suspicious, so I got the guys to check the car out this morning as a priority. It was quite a mess, but they found that the brake pipes had been cut to both front wheels. It looks like it was deliberately sabotaged, which is why we want this to be a murder investigation. My boss will contact yours, but I thought you'd want the details asap."

"Yes, that is very helpful, thank you", responded Webb. "Is the vehicle over at your team's yard? I want to come and see for myself."

"Yes, you are welcome. I've brought you the paper file with all the details so far, plus print outs of the photographs. They will come digitally via e-mail when your boss has officially accepted the case," added Richards, "but I have taken the liberty of bringing some of the chaps' personal effects – phone, wallet, keys, and so on. I understand that the Coroner has already requested a full autopsy."

"That's excellent," commented Ron. "I'm glad your observation skills made you suspicious; otherwise, the saboteur might have got away with it."

"Not much chance of that now, sir," grinned Dave. "When I was with Peggy, it seemed that you cracked most cases within a week."

"Well, we do our best, but some cases take much longer. Anyway, thank you again, and please give my regards to your boss, Albert Barnard. We trained together." The phrase clearly dismissed Richards, who left through the general office. "Cheerio", he called over to Peggy, but she pretended not to hear him.

Morris Murder

Chapter 3

Friday, 10th March, 2017

Ron studied the folder briefly before gathering the team around him. He told them all he knew about the case, and DS Catchpole wrote up critical facts on the whiteboard as he spoke. There wasn't much to go on. "I'm keeping the photographs for the time being," he explained. "I want to visit the crash site and to look at the cut brake pipes. DS Catchpole, you are welcome to come with me. When the file is sent through e-mail, you can put copies up here, together with pictures of any key characters you can obtain. I have got the parents' addresses. DC Winter, see if you can find me an address for these morris men, plus any background on them. DC Cateby, get all you can on the victim. We have his wallet and phone, so let's see if you can find his phone contacts, bank account, etc. DC Corcoran, your favourite job!"

"CCTV, sir?" Jim Corcoran sighed.

"Yes, there may not be much, seeing as it is a country area, but find what you can, including any of these fancy new camera doorbells people are getting. You need to track from where the morris practice happened to the crash site, but you may also have to do some door knocking for eye-witnesses," Webb confirmed.

"Unavoidably, we have lost nearly 24 hours on this case before it has come to us. At the moment, the public and press do not know that it is anything other than a tragic accident. That means the killer may still think they got away with it. That means we need to pick up speed quickly, so sadly, you may need to cancel some weekend plans. Give your partners a call to warn them. Being a weekend, we should be able to catch people at home instead of them being at work. My first thought was that the murderer was someone who knew Archie and where he would be on a Thursday night. It's a cowardly approach to kill someone: not having to face them as they die. Obviously, it had to be preplanned and not a spur-of-the-moment incident by someone who didn't care whether anyone else got injured when the car went out of control. Any questions? Right, let's get busy!"

Chris Winter left an ansaphone message for his girlfriend Juliet, the court usher. They had only recently moved in together. "Hi Juliet, you know how I said I sometimes have to work odd hours at short notice? Sorry, but a case has just come in, and I will be late tonight and working tomorrow. I'll bring fish and chips on my way home for us."

Will Cateby rang Gloria at her shipping office and caught her before she left work. They didn't live together yet and had planned to visit

Lavenham on Saturday but agreed to postpone it. Jim Corcoran spoke to his mother, with whom he lived, to let her know he would be home late and working the next day. "I'll leave your dinner on a plate to microwave for when you get in, dear," his mother replied. Now, you be careful and stay safe!"

Jim said goodbye and reflected that if he had wanted to 'be careful and stay safe', he wouldn't have joined the police! The only person not having to consider other people was Peggy, who would only have a lazy weekend at home anyway. She got her coat on and waited for Ron to ring his long-suffering wife, Alice. They set out for the vehicle compound in Ron's Rover. They had to pass a large, locked compound of impounded cars on the way in. They were the ones impounded for being driven illegally, awaiting collection by their owners. Beyond that, there were three ranks of vehicles parked in lines. Not every car there was wrecked. Some were awaiting forensic searches for evidence of crimes, but the mangled red Ford Fiesta made a sad centrepiece on a hoist in the garage behind them. A technician in overalls called Terry showed them the cut brake pipes leading to the front wheels.

"If you look closely, you'll see that where they have been cut through, the pipes have crushed first," he explained. "That suggests whatever cut

Morris Murder

them wasn't very sharp. Most pipes are made of a copper-nickel alloy nowadays. They are less susceptible to corrosion, although sometimes steel is used. Since they have been cut from above and below, it suggests that something like a pair of pliers was used. Because the ends have partly crimped together, the brake fluid will not have drained out straight away, although it will not have been working the brakes. So, the driver will have initially got some resistance when he pushed the brake pedal, although it wasn't having any effect. The system is fairly dry now, so the fluid had probably mostly gone by the time of the crash. I understand it was only a short distance from where he started, so he may not have even realised he had a problem until then, especially if he didn't use the brakes much."

"I understand it was a country road without much traffic on it," commented Ron. "Any fingerprints?"

"No recent ones. Some places on the sill appear to have been gripped, probably to pull the saboteur's body from underneath. However, they are flat without much detail, so there is no joy there. Inevitably, they wore gloves. There is one faint ray of hope, though: if you look at the nearside brake pipe, there is a tiny spot of green near the cut. We think it may be from the gloves that were worn, caught on the sharp edge. That or it could be from clothing" He shone his torch at the pipe.

"Ah, yes, I see it," said Peggy.

"We are going to take the sections of the cut pipe off for further analysis. A garage mechanic could have even left it," concluded Terry. "Two of the tyres looked new, and the rest of the car was in a reasonable condition before the crash. I checked, and it had only recently had an MOT. The airbag had deployed."

"Well, thank you very much for that," said Ron. "Seeing something always makes it clearer than an official report." After thanking Terry once more and urging that the forensic analysis be done quickly, Ron left with Peggy for the scene of the accident. It was getting late in the afternoon, and they wanted to see it in what was left of the winter daylight. Seeing the wrecked car was a sombre sight, and the detectives carried on to the A14 towards Bury St Edmunds without saying much. Ron instinctively reached for his unending supply of humbugs and offered one to Peggy.

Turning off the A14 brought them quickly into Woolpit. They passed through the attractive marketplace, bordered by timber-framed houses and shops from the 14th and 15th centuries. In a central triangle, an ornate pump house has a grotesque face carved on its wooden frame of four pillars, surmounted by a conical tiled roof. They had no time to pause and admire the place as Ron headed the car for the crash site. He was using his sat-nav, but Peggy had extracted the map book from the pocket in the car door. "There is more than one way to go to Walsham le Willows, but we need the route that travels via Elmswell," Ron nodded.

The place where Archie had died was quite evident. Tyre tracks crossed the verge, and lumps of bark had freshly fallen from the trunk of an oak tree. The verge had also been churned up by the wheels of emergency services at its edge to the road. Ron parked a little bit past it so that his car was in a safe, visible place, and the pair of detectives got out to look closer.

"It's not even a particularly tight bend," commented Peggy.

"I agree with you," confirmed Ron. "The car was going fast enough to cross the verge without getting bogged down in it and hard enough to damage the tree." There wasn't much more to be said or done, so they climbed back in their car and headed to Archie's parents in Walsham le Willows. The door was opened by Mr Berry, who hardly glanced at their warrant cards before inviting them in. Mrs Berry sat in an armchair, and from the look of her tear-stained face and tightly held tissue, she had obviously been crying.

"It seems so little to say in a situation like this, but we are truly sorry for your loss," opened Ron. "Was he your only child?"

"Yes, he was," replied Mr Berry. "You don't expect a son to die before a parent, do you?"

"No indeed," consoled Ron. "What was he like?"

"Archie was a decent chap. We worked together at Badwell Ash Garden Centre & Nursery. I am the general manager, and he had a Saturday job there before leaving school and then full-time since he was 16. He manages the shop side of the operation for me. He has never been in trouble with the police, and I thought he was a reasonable driver. I gave him that car for his 21st birthday. It had been mine, and I bought myself a new one. It only had its MOT about six weeks ago and passed OK other than buying two new tyres, so there shouldn't have been anything wrong with it."

Mrs Berry was snivelling and got up from her chair. "I'll make us some tea," she half whispered.

When she had moved into the kitchen, her husband added quietly, "It has hit us both very hard, but Avril especially. He was her pride and joy, and she could never see a fault in him."

Taking this as a cue, Ron asked quietly, "None of us are perfect. Did he have any faults, do you think?"

Mr Berry hesitated, then said, "He was a bit too keen on going out roistering and enjoying himself to my mind, especially with the young ladies. I used to have to push him to save some money. I have always been more of a home-loving man."

As Mrs Berry re-entered with a tea tray, Peggy tried to engage her with a follow-up question: "Did Archie have a particular girlfriend that he was close to?"

"No, and he never brought anyone home here. I wanted him to find a nice girl, settle down and give me grandchildren before I got too old. He was 23 years old, you know. He was popular, but nothing seemed to last very long," she added. "Cecil and I were married by his age."

"What about other friends?" Ron asked.

"He had his pals at Woolpit Morris. That's where he had been, for a practice at Woolpit Village Hall on Thursday night. We went to see them perform last Summer in the village. He was an excellent dancer," exclaimed Cecil Berry proudly. "Other than that, nobody else, as far as I know. His best friends from his school days moved

Morris Murder

away from the area. Pardon me for asking, but why are you so interested in who else he knew?"

"Well, I was coming to that," replied Webb. "We are looking into the possibility that his car may have been tampered with. Now, don't get me wrong, it may not have been, but we have to check these things out. Was there anybody that Archie had clashed with at work or around the village?"

"No, he has always got on with people alright. The customers certainly seemed to like him at work, but we brought him up to be polite and pleasant with people," Cecil explained.

"Who could do that to my darling boy?" was the anguished cry from Avril. "He has never done anyone any harm." She started sobbing, and Peggy went over to comfort her and hand her a fresh tissue.

Cecil said that the business owner had given him a few days off. "We will visit there as well to see if there is anything else we can find out," said Ron. "I will be talking to his morris dancing friends as well. We shall make every effort. Do you know how to contact them?"

"No, I don't, I'm afraid," responded Mr Berry. "I know Archie mentioned that they had a new leader recently, but I don't know if he even mentioned his name."

"Would it be alright to check his room?" enquired Ron. "There may be a note there of them or his other friends."

"Yes, that is alright, but please do not disturb anything, please," requested Avril Berry, who had managed to stop crying for a moment. "I want it left just how he had it."

Assuring her they would take care of it, the two detectives went upstairs. There was very little personal stuff in Archie's room besides a computer games console, tv and clothes. They checked the chest of draws but found nothing but clothes. On top of it was a couple of opened bottles of aftershave and a music magazine. Shaking his head, Ron said, "Let's head home."

On the way back to Martlesham HQ, Ron was sucking on his usual humbug, and Peggy was watching the dusky landscape pass by through the window. She was thinking about Dave's visit to the office. He could have e-mailed everything, but he seemed to want to visit. It felt like an intrusion, and he had never been there when they were together. She didn't regret treating him coldly and didn't want to encourage him to contact her again. It was hard enough trying to start a new life without complications from the past, and she wasn't about to forgive him for cheating on her. Suddenly, she was aware that her governor was speaking. "Sorry, I missed that," she apologised.

"I forgot to tell you about my meeting with His Lordship this morning."

"Oh, did he have anything interesting to say?"

"Well, it started badly. He mentioned the SCS, and it was several minutes before I realised that he was talking about us! It sounded like one of those furniture warehouses that advertise on TV."

"Ha! He loves his acronyms – Serious Crime Squad, SCS. It could have been worse. He might have wanted to have renamed us something entirely ridiculous in line with some new politically correct missive from above."

"Yes, the Naughty People Service or something!" Ron chuckled. "Anyway, he was enquiring about each of the team members. I could see him cribbing from a list – he never has known any of them very well. Apart from you, that is, he had been impressed with your handling of the Hadleigh case in my absence and all the other stuff you have done. So have I, and I told him so."

"Thank you, sir," acknowledged Peggy.

"Yes, he suggested I forward your name for the firearms course. I'm the only authorised officer in our squad, and it would all count towards any future career progression. How would you feel about that?" he asked.

"Well, I'm glad that as a Police Force, we aren't permanently armed like some of those abroad. Yet there are times when it is necessary, regrettable as that may be. Frankly, I don't know if I could shoot someone. I wouldn't know for certain until the situation confronted me, but if they were pointing a gun at me, then better them dead than myself." Peggy wondered if she had said too much or even the wrong thing. She knew that attitude was more looked at than ability in selecting armed officers.

"It seems you have the same attitude as myself," reassured Ron. "I have been assigned a firearm for years now. I have only drawn it a few times and never fired it other than on a range. Whilst there have been certain criminals, I would have loved to have been dead, I still don't really know whether I could do it. What I never intended to do was be some sort of gung-ho hero. If I suspect that there may be weapons at a place, I call in the ARU[2] as a precaution. They are trained and experienced to deal with those situations more safely and professionally. I suppose there may always be an incident where

---

[2] ARU Armed Response Unit

a gun is produced unexpectedly, and there is no opportunity to call in the heavy brigade. You would find that the course deals as much with the psychological questions as it does on how to shoot straight."

"That's comforting to know, sir, and thank you for sharing your experience. I think, on balance, I would like to be put forward for the course, please," Peggy announced.

"So long as you don't use the gun on your ex!" Ron joked. "Seriously, I don't want him bothering you at work. I shall deter any further visits," Webb added darkly. Ron changed the subject without wishing to be drawn on what he had just said. "Of course, the annual appraisements are coming up soon, which is what His Lordship was on about. I'd appreciate your thoughts on the rest of the team as their DS, in confidence, of course."

"Fair enough," commented Peggy. "That should be part of my role, helping with appraisements. Firstly, I don't think I have any problems with any of them. They all work hard and contribute in their own ways, and morale is good, which inevitably comes from cracking cases together. One thing I do think we could consider in their development, though, is moving tasks around."

"Yes, go on," Ron encouraged.

"Well, for example, Will Cateby. He is superb at tracking and analysing bank accounts, social media, etc. I fear he may be stuck in that mode because he is the obvious choice to do those tasks. Maybe we could get him to mentor another team member to be as good as him and release him to get out of the office occasionally to interview witnesses?"

"That's a good point. We can't have officers getting bored or indispensable. Giving a task to the person who is best at it is too easy. If they are absent, we need someone to take their place. How about the others?"

"I took Chris Winter with me when I handled the Hadleigh case, and he was getting into the swing of doing my usual tasks. Maybe you could take him along instead of me sometime in the future and give him some tips. I can see him applying for his sergeant's exam before too long, especially now that he has settled down and moved in with his girlfriend."

"Yes, you could be right. If you go further, as I hope you will eventually, I'll need a replacement. Incidentally, Winter did not pass the firearms course he went onto last year, so it's best not to say too much about it in front of him. What about our newest member, Jim Corcoran? He seems keen, which is why I pinched him from uniform, but he is mainly our CCTV expert at present."

"There is a lot of hard slog, sitting through hours of film, looking for one clue, and he certainly sticks to it quite methodically. I must admit, I haven't got to know him quite as well as the others. He seems to keep himself to himself a bit more. Maybe we need to make him Will Cateby's apprentice?" Peggy suggested.

"Yes, that certainly bears thinking about," commented Ron. "Oh well, here's the carpark. I can drop you by your car if you do not need to go inside."

"That will be smashing," Peggy replied brightly. "Thank you, sir and goodnight."

Morris Murder

Chapter 4

Saturday, 11th March, 2017

The morning began with a catch-up on what had been learned so far by individual members of the Serious Crime Squad. Ron told them what they had found out yesterday, and Peggy wrote up salient points on the board. A picture of Archie had been downloaded from his driving license record and stuck with his name at the top of the information.

"There is no telephone number, website or e-mail listed for Woolpit Morris," announced DC Winter. "I have found a name and address for 'The Squire', which is what they call their leader. His name is Bob Spurgeon, and he lives in Woolpit. That is from a local folk organisers website that hasn't been updated for about 18 months, but it was the only thing I could find."

"The parents did say that there was a new leader, but if Bob Spurgeon were the old one, he would surely know who took over from him," reasoned Peggy Catchpole.

"Yes, I think we should make a visit there today. Hopefully, we can get a list of other members and interview them over the weekend while most will be off work," decided Ron. "The parents said that the morris group practised at Woolpit Village Hall. I want to take a look at it because that is

Morris Murder

the most likely place for the sabotage to have taken place. DC Corcoran that gives you a start point for the fateful car journey. Any luck with any CCTV footage yet?"

"No sir," responded Corcoran. "There aren't any official cameras at all in the village. I found references to some on a couple of business addresses, but they may not cover the right area. I will go out and trace the route on foot to check for private CCTV on houses and knock on any doors of houses overlooking the village hall."

"Good," agreed Ron. "How about you, DC Cateby?"

"As you said, he works at Bardwell Ash Garden Centre and receives a regular wage from there. He seems to spend most of it but saves £100 per month in a second account. He has also deposited two sums of £100 into it. There is about £10,000 in that account, but most of it has come from a single deposit last December. It was a cheque from a solicitor and appears to be from a relative's will. About a month later, he drew £1000 out in cash. I'd like to find out what for. You say he already has a car, and a holiday would usually be paid for by cheque or credit card. It may be entirely innocent, but I think it is worth chasing up."

"Yes, we don't like mysteries or anomalies. Keep at it!" encouraged Ron.

"I found out that he had a Facebook page as well," reported Will Cateby. He doesn't seem to use it much, but I could see he belongs to a closed group for Woolpit Morris. I couldn't get access yesterday, but I will apply to our tech guys if it is essential. His phone was locked, so I have already sent that to them. I will search for all the other social media sites today."

With that, the meeting broke up, and soon, Ron and Peggy returned to Woolpit. Jim Corcoran followed quickly afterwards.

Woolpit Village Hall was unusual in that it had two storeys. An exterior wooden staircase at the front accessed the upper level. Ron pulled his Rover into the large, concrete carpark and exited the car with Peggy.

"I wonder if anyone else was using the other part of the hall?" queried Peggy.

"That would be very handy since there are windows facing onto the carpark. I doubt we will be that lucky, though," Ron pessimistically responded. "Who else would want the sound of music and stomping feet disturbing their own activities?" They wandered over to a notice board, which didn't give details of who occupied the place on particular nights. Down the side of the hall, they could see a playing field, a children's playground and the church in the distance. To each side of the car park were high

Morris Murder

fences with homes on the other side of them, plus another white house on the opposite side of the road. Jim Corcoran then turned up and parked his Mini alongside Ron's car. Ron waited for him to get out, then indicated the houses. "They look worth checking out first", he instructed. We'll see you later."

Back in the car, Webb and Catchpole made their way to the address in Woolpit that had been found for the Squire of Woolpit Morris, Bob Spurgeon. It turned out to be a modest mid-terraced house with white painted walls and a slate roof. There was a long pause after Peggy knocked on the door, but they could hear feint sounds of someone coming, so they waited patiently with warrant cards in hand. The door was opened by a grizzled-looking, bearded older man supported by a walking frame. They introduced themselves, and he welcomed them in. "I don't get many visitors now, so come and sit down." He had a slightly grubby cardigan and jogger trousers on, but his mouth drooped to one side noticeably, slurring his speech. He looked up at them under wildly bushy eyebrows. "How can I help you?" he asked.

"Am I right in thinking you are the Squire of Woolpit Morris?" Ron asked.

"Unfortunately not," came the reply. "When I had this stroke, I had to hand it over to someone

Morris Murder

else. I had to retire from being an agricultural engineer as well, damn it. Harry Scrivener is the new Squire. He only lives along the street from here, but I saw him going out with his wife only 10 minutes ago. I expect they've gone shopping, so they'll probably be half an hour or so. We should see them pass by the window on their way back. Anything I can help you with?"

"What we need most of all is a list of everyone at the rehearsal last Thursday night, but other than that, any background you could give us would be helpful, Mr Spurgeon, please," requested Ron. Peggy had discreetly pulled out her notebook.

"Harry can give you the address list – I passed it on to him. He helped me start the side a few years ago. We were in Hageneth Morris, another local side, but there was a bit of a clash of personalities, so some of us left to form Woolpit Morris. We have had other people join us since then. You need younger members coming up to replace old codgers like me, but it has caused a few problems."

"What sort of problems?" prompted Ron.

"Well, we are known for dancing the Cotswold traditions of morris dance, keeping to a local area of villages. Some of the new members have wanted to go further afield, to folk festivals and the like. That means travelling and camping, something some older members are averse to.

35

Also, some of them were keen to do other winter activities, like Molly dancing, an East Anglian Tradition that has become more popular. Still, there is already a mixed Molly side in Bury St Edmunds, Milkmaid Molly they're called. We have usually practised in winter and then had our first appearance on May 1st, going through to September. They might be able to exist side by side, but I can foresee divided loyalties. You can always tell our side: we have white shirts and trousers, green bell pads on our legs and crossed green baldricks across our chests with a badge of the Green Children since we are based in Woolpit."

"I saw a big village sign on the way in, with them and a wolf on it. What's the significance of that to Woolpit?" asked Peggy since they appeared to have time to kill before the current Squire returned.

"Oh, you'll see in some books that Woolpit refers to a wolf pit. It's a load of bunkum! I am a member of the Woolpit History Society. The most likely explanation is that it came from the personal name of Ulfketel, which, when translated from Old English, means wolf (ulf) trap (ketel)). Ulfketel Snillenger was a famous warrior and is often referred to as the Earl of the Eastern Angles, so it would not be surprising to find a village named after him. The Green Children, though, is a lovely story." Before they could stop him and get back to questions, he was off, clearly delighted to have a new audience for the tale.

"A girl and a boy with green-tinged skin were found in the fields near Woolpit by some villagers at harvest time centuries ago. No one could understand their language, so they were taken to Sir Richard de Calne at Wikes Hall, six miles away at Bardwell. They seemed hungry but wouldn't eat anything until they saw a servant carrying some green beans through the hall. When they were given the beans, they devoured them instantly, raw and pods and all!

The boy, the younger of the two, was always lethargic and eventually died. The girl survived, her green colour faded, and they reckon she married a man from King's Lynn. As she got older, she learned the local language and said she and her brother had gotten lost looking for a stray sheep. The legend was first written down by a monk called Ralph of Coggeshall and another one named William of Newburgh. Of course, it is only a legend, but I've been told that severe iron deficiency due to lack of meat in the diet can produce anaemia, which in turn causes tiredness and a greenish tinge to the skin."

"What a charming tale," said Ron. "Now tell me about this new Squire we are waiting for."

Morris Murder

Spurgeon rubbed his chin thoughtfully before speaking. "The trouble is, Harry is a nice chap, but he's worried about upsetting anybody. They elected him, and he feels he must sit on the fence for fear of offending either opinion. You can't run a side like that! Anyway, how come the police are suddenly interested in Morris dancing? Are you putting on an event or wanting us to stop dancing in the road?"

"Neither really, Mr Spurgeon, although it is all fascinating," responded Ron. "Unfortunately, a member of Woolpit morris was killed in a car crash last Thursday night on the way home from practice."

"Oh no, who was it?"

"Archie Berry. There is a possibility that his car may have been tampered with. That is not confirmed, but of course, we have to look into it."

"So you are wondering whether a member might have messed with his motor? No, they may disagree from time to time, but I can't see any of them upset enough to do that!" exclaimed Bob excitedly. "That Archie was a good dancer and well-liked. He might even have become Squire himself one day. What a waste." Just then, a couple walked past the window. "There's Harry and his wife Maureen now, carrying the shopping back. They'll be going back to number 23."

Chapter 5

Saturday, 11th March, 2017

Ron and Peggy rapidly gave their thanks and goodbyes and hurried up the street. They caught up with the couple as they unlocked the front door. "Hello, police. When you have put your shopping away, we'd like a word, please. We've just been talking to your friend Bob, and he pointed you out," explained Ron. Harry Scrivener looked slightly startled but invited them in. He was a wiry individual in his forties, with a few wisps of hair on either side of his bald head and a snub nose surmounted with a pair of owl-like spectacles. He removed his coat to reveal a chunky green sweater and brown corduroy trousers. His wife absented herself into the kitchen on the pretext of putting the shopping away and making a pot of tea. They sat around a square wooden table. Ron explained why they were calling, and Harry was quite shocked.

"No, I don't believe it! I heard that there was a car accident last Thursday night but didn't dream it was him. He was still talking to his friend Neville Rands when I left. Maureen!" he called to his wife. Young Archie was in that accident on Thursday night. He was killed!"

When the tea had been brought in, and Maureen had carried on about young men racing around in cars for a bit, Ron tried to break the news gently that sabotage may have been involved. "We cannot say for sure, but we cannot rule out that Archie's car may have been fiddled with in the carpark outside the hall. Of course, we must follow that up, so I want to speak to everyone who was there. Do you have a membership list, please?"

"Yes, you can have mine," Harry offered and went to a draw to find it. He handed it over. "I can print myself out another one from the computer." He nodded towards an aged PC and printer in the corner. "Is it ok if I notify everyone on the Facebook page? It is a closed group, so nobody else will see it."

"Can I ask you to wait until Monday, please, Mr Scrivener?" asked Ron. "We don't want people jumping to conclusions at this stage." Harry nodded.

"Was everyone on this list there last Thursday night?" asked Peggy, who had taken charge of it.

"Everyone except Wilky Wilkinson. He has to work some evenings at Ipswich Docks, so he is not always available for practices. Otherwise, everyone else was present."

"Does anybody else use the hall at the same time?" continued Peggy, remembering the second storey.

"No, we are probably a bit too noisy. Fortunately, the houses are far enough away from the hall so as not to disturb them," explained Harry.

"I understand that you only recently took over the side?" asked Ron, trying to get more into the dynamics of the group.

"Yes, it was quite an honour when they elected me after poor old Bob Spurgeon had his stroke. He was very dedicated, but I am starting to realise that it is a bit of a poisoned chalice!"

"Why is that?" encouraged Ron, feigning ignorance.

"Well, some of us older members started Woolpit Morris after leaving Hageneth Morris. We are happy to commit to dancing Cotswold-type Morris around the local area. However, some younger members want to up the standard and perform at national folk festivals. Archie supported that. Some are even keen to perform another tradition in winter, such as Molly or Border. With the different ideas floating around and the death of Archie, an incident like this could finish the side,

Sorry, I should explain: Cotswold is the hanky and stick dances collected from villages in the Cotswolds, usually done with white outfits, bell pads on the legs and crossed baldricks on the chest. Ours are green, with the Woolpit legend of the Green Children in a rosette in the middle. Each side is different, and some wear straw boaters or even caps.

Molly is an East Anglian winter tradition that has been revived in recent years. They usually paint their faces and have a variety of outfits. Border Morris comes from the Welsh Borders and Northwest from the North-West of England. They dance quite differently, and some wear clogs. Green Dragon from Bury St Edmunds is a mixed Border side, and then there is Hoxon Hundred mixed Cotswold. Sorry, I seem to be getting into a lecture here!"

"That's OK, it is fascinating. I had no idea there were so many varieties or groups in one small area. There must be a lot of people involved," exclaimed Ron. "So, getting back to your people, I guess it caused some tensions."

"Yes, but not serious enough to cause one of them to sabotage another man's car!" defended Harry. "We all get on pretty well most of the time. If someone felt really strongly, they would probably leave and join another side. There are plenty of them around Suffolk. East Suffolk Morris in Ipswich is huge and even tours abroad. They have very high standards. Old Glory Molly from Rumburgh is one of the most admired Molly sides in the UK, and other groups perform various traditions. There is even a rapper sword dance team called Old School over at Horham, near Eye. There are plenty of groups for dancers to choose from."

"I see," said Webb. "You said that Archie and his friend were the last to leave. Who else would have been left?"

"Just the musicians. They take a little longer to pack their stuff away. Billy Newson always locks up. We have our own key. He also opens up for us so the musicians can practice a little before the dancers arrive. Last Thursday, I was next in because I walked from here since it's not too far. The rest turned up within about ten minutes. I try to keep them punctual!"

"Do they have a break during the evening?" enquired Webb.

"Yes, at around 9 pm. It gives them a chance to catch their breath, drink some water and so on, but they can slip out between dances for the toilet or just to get a breath of fresh air. There are a couple of smokers who slip outside for a crafty drag. I generally give out notices during the break about where we are visiting, etc.

"What was Archie like?" asked Ron.

"A good dancer and popular with the lads as far as I could tell. He was a 'bit of a lad', and we will miss him."

"What do you mean a bit of a lad?"

"Well, he was young and single with an eye for the ladies by all accounts, but one shouldn't talk ill of the dead. He was very friendly with Neil Rands, a black chap who joined the side."

"Is that unusual?" queried Ron. "I have never thought about there being black morris dancers before."

"Oh yes, it's not common, but there are a few. He has fitted in very well, a nice chap."

"So, there isn't anybody you might think that had a grudge against Archie?"

"No, not at all. His poor parents! He was their only son. I met them last summer when we danced at Walsham le Willows."

Webb glanced over to Catchpole, who discreetly shook her head to indicate that she had nothing more to ask. He quickly made their goodbyes, and the detectives returned to their car, parked outside Bob Spurgeon's house. They could see him hunched over in his chair through the window, but he did not notice them return to the car.

"I can see what Bob meant by Harry not wanting to offend anyone. What did you think?" asked Peggy.

"Uneasy lies the head that wears a crown", quoted Webb.[3] "I think he was being honest, but it is bad news that people could leave the hall anytime and return without suspicion."

"Yes, I have been thinking about that," ventured Peggy. "I reckon it would be a bit risky sabotaging the car at the start of the evening unless you were certain you were the last to arrive. Otherwise, someone else turning up could see you."

"Unless you hid between the cars, particularly if you could manage to park your own beside Archies," countered Ron.

"Yes, I can concede that," said Peggy, "but it still seems less likely that someone would get seen if they left the hall during the evening to have a cigarette, go to the loo or get some fresh air."

Having exhausted that topic for the moment, the pair perused the list of contact details they had been given. Colin (Clacky) Clark also lived in Woolpit, so they decided he should be their next target.

Colin lived in a house not far from the ancient church of the Blessed Virgin Mary. It is much visited by people wanting to see the wooden angels in the roof and the bench ends carved

---

[3] King Henry the Fourth, Part Two, by William Shakespeare

into birds and animals. Notably, there is a carved stone woodwose that has become detached from the structure.[4] 19-year-old Colin had never seen any of this despite living nearby. He merely moaned about visitors' cars parked along the road by his home, which made it more difficult to tear around on his Honda 90cc motorbike. Ron's motor was added to the line of cards.

Mrs Clark answered the door, and the police presented their credentials. "Is Colin at home, please?" asked DS Catchpole.

"Yes, what has he been up to?" snapped his seemingly harassed Mum.

"Nothing as far as we know. He is not in trouble. We just want him to help us out with some information, please," said Webb, trying to allay her fears. She yelled up the stairs that led from the small hallway, and on the second call, he appeared and came down. He wore an overlarge tee-shirt with a Japanese Manga design and distressed jeans. His hair was long enough to touch his shoulders and hung in lank locks that he habitually swept away from his face.

"What is it?" he challenged.

---

[4] Woodwose are wild man figures with clubs, particularly found in 14th century Suffolk churches. For a complete guide see *The Woodwose in Suffolk & beyond.* By Pete Jennings – Gruff (2019)

Morris Murder

"It's the police. Now show some manners and invite them into the living room instead of leaving them out on the step for all the neighbours to see," admonished his obviously irritated Mother. Once inside, Webb explained why they were there.

"Yeah, of course, I know him. He seemed a bit of a posh boy to me. I wouldn't have wished him dead, but I weren't keen on him. It was bad enough being constantly corrected by the old Squire Bob. Harry, the new one, is more relaxed, but then Archie also started trying to correct my steps. *'The half galley should come straight off the Hey, without a step in between',* he mimicked. Bloody know-all!"

"Language!" snapped Mrs Clark. "Less of that Art School attitude around here!"

"Yes, Mum," mumbled Clacky, dipping his head down.

"So, what attracted a young chap like you to join a morris side?" asked Ron pleasantly, hoping to lighten up the mood a bit.

"My art school buddies are in Ipswich, and I've never been into running and sport. It's good to have a bunch of blokes you can go for a pint and have a laugh with. It even keeps you fit if you can avoid the beer belly! I'm proud to be English, and we are good at our daft traditions, aren't we?"

"Yes, I agree with you there," replied Ron. They didn't get much out of him after that, so they left. "My tummy is telling me it's lunchtime, and I spotted a teashop back down the road. Shall we?" asked Ron.

"Definitely!" replied Peggy enthusiastically. "It is probably as easy to walk than park down there," she commented, so they did. It was a tiny place on the village square, beside the museum and village institute entrance.

Two splendid bacon sandwiches and mugs of tea later, they felt ready to face some more morris men. "We can visit his work colleagues tomorrow at Badwell Ash, but let's catch Neville Rands at Walsham le Willows. He seems to have been the closest friend to him in the group and the last to see him alive," decided Ron.

On the way there, Peggy told Ron the one thing she knew about Walsham-le-Willows. "There is a special thing in the church there. I remember reading about it somewhere recently. She got out her phone and searched the internet. "Ah, here it is. I thought it was rather quaint and charming. 'There is a carved wooden medallion from what was called a maiden's crant, which was a flower garland. (There is a little picture of both sides of it.) It commemorates Mary Boyce, who died at twenty years old of a broken heart on the 15th of November 1685. The garland was a symbol of her virginity, and they put them up for all such young ladies."

"Not much call for them nowadays," remarked Ron sardonically."

"Not a romantic then, sir?" responded Peggy, chuckling.

"Still, you sound like you go in for some interesting reading matter," Ron commented.

"I like books about East Anglia, whether they are history, folklore or fiction. Do you read much?"

"Not a great deal, but when I do, I still love the old Hornblower series by CS Forester. It's great historical stuff with a human angle. Reading detective fiction is too much like work!" Ron quipped.

"I know what you mean," sympathised Peggy. "So many of those old ones rely on a dropped object or false identity. If only crooks made it that easy! Solving everything by DNA, mobile phones, and CCTV will make more modern ones a bit boring and repetitive."

"Don't worry. I think they will still need us to ask the right questions and make connections. Well, until they get robots to do it!"

They soon arrived at Rand's home in Walsham le Willows.

Chapter 6

Saturday, 11th March, 2017

Neville Rands appeared at the door in a vest and jeans. He was 20 years old and had cropped curly hair with stubble on his chin above a broad smile of gleaming teeth. He leant on the doorframe with bare arms of muscular, gleaming dark skin, looking quizzical. "My mother is at work today," he said.

"Ah, it is you we'd like to talk to, Neville," replied Peggy, holding up her warrant card. "We are police. May we come in, please?" He didn't answer but turned and led them inside.

"What's this about?" he asked, a little suspiciously.

"It's about Archie Berry, your friend from Woolpit Morris. I'm sorry to tell you that he died in a car accident last Thursday night. It seems that you were probably the last person to see him alive," announced Ron.

"No! Surely not?" It took a moment or two for the information to sink in, and he looked shocked. "Yes, we were talking afterwards. He was trying to show me the special Bledington 'hook leg' turn. Then I got into my car, and I presume he followed me back to Walsham soon after. How did it happen?"

"Well, we are still trying to establish that, but he went off at a bend into a tree just outside Woolpit," responded Webb. "How was he when you left him?"

"Fine. Archie was laughing, actually. I had tried to do the move and nearly fell over! He was his usual cheery self. All the side have made me welcome, but he has become my best friend there, probably because we are of a similar age group. I don't; sorry, I didn't see him much outside Woolpit Morris, but he regularly attends the weekly practice or dance outs. Although we live in the same place, he works at a local garden centre, but I am a telephone engineer over at Stowmarket."

"I understand that having a black Morris dancer is a little unusual. Does that cause you any problems?" asked Peggy.

"No, they are a good bunch of chaps, and I like the idea of men dancing together and having fun. It keeps us fit, as well. I suppose you have to be slightly eccentric to do what they do, so me being a little different is no bother. Funnily enough, there have been some arguments about traditional dance sides who black their faces, being called inappropriate. Everyone in the folk world knows that historically, it was to disguise the faces with the handiest thing to hand, which was soot. It is all a load of rubbish! I don't find it offensive at all – it's just history, innit?

If the men think that I am different, it is probably more due to my drinking habits. A lot of the dancing takes place around pubs, and I am happy to go in with them, but I usually have a Coca-Cola. They can't make out why I don't like beer! It is probably my mother's doing. Daddy drank himself to death when I was little, so she has put me off alcohol. She has had to work hard by herself to bring me up and moved us here from London. She is out now, looking after older people in their homes as a Carer. She got me educated, and I passed an apprenticeship."

"Being a telecoms engineer is a very worthwhile career. I suppose you have to deal with the internet and telephones nowadays?" commented Webb. "Commuting from here to Stowmarket on apprentice wages must have been a struggle."

"Yes, it was. The buses aren't exactly regular if I couldn't cadge a lift. Archie lent me the money to buy a little car when I qualified. I hadn't been able to save much money, but I think he inherited some from a relative, his Grandad. Archie reckoned he got feeble interest from the bank, so he let me have £1000. That's the sort of friend he was. I have been paying him back £100 monthly on my new wages. The idea is that I will give him back an extra payment so he will make £100, or 10% of it. That is far more than the interest that he gets and far less than I would have had to pay for a bank loan, assuming that I could even get one. I insisted on signing an IOU and so on. He said it was a good investment on money he didn't need right now. I don't know what will happen now. I know he said he didn't want his father to know."

"I'm afraid I can't help you there; it is a bit outside of my legal knowledge," admitted Webb. The detectives left soon after this since Neville seemed to have given them a lot of information.

"Well, his honesty saves DC Cateby from chasing around after those payments," said Catchpole when they returned to the car. "Shall I give him a call?"

"Yes, do that, please," decided Webb, selecting another humbug. "Check and see if there is anything else interesting that they have found out as well."

Cateby answered the phone, and Peggy updated him. "Ah, thanks for that. That has saved me a lengthy job trying to find out about the £1000 cash withdrawal. DC Corcoran has just got back in. I don't think he has found any useful CCTV or witnesses, I'm afraid. The lab has just been through to say that they have extracted the mobile phone messages, and I am just about to be sent a list of calls from the provider."

"What about DC Winter?" asked Peggy.

"Hang on," there was a pause while Cateby shouted across the room to Winter. "No criminal records for anyone so far, but he still has many of them to check."

"OK, thanks. I guess there isn't too much for you to do tomorrow, so we'll see you on Monday. Come back with some fresh ideas!" commanded Peggy. Ron had been listening on the speakerphone and nodded.

"What did you make of Neville Rands then? Ron asked.

"He seemed a bit anti when we turned up, but maybe he has had bad experiences with police in the past. He ended up volunteering a lot, though," opined Peggy.

"Call me suspicious, but was he trying to cover himself about that loan," grumbled Webb. "Was there more to it than that? He would expect someone to look at Archie's bank account after he died, so it was best to get in his story first before questions were asked. What if he had been trying to avoid paying the rest back? People have been killed for less!"

"True," admitted Catchpole. "I guess we will have to leave him as a possible suspect. I noticed that you didn't tell him foul play was suspected. I presume that was deliberate?"

"Yes, he will find out soon enough when they get talking to each other. I thought he was enough on his guard, and I didn't want him to get defensive and clam up. Now, there was another Morris man who lived around Walsham-le-Willows, I think. Ah yes, Paul Hicks. Let me put the postcode into my Sat-Nav."

Hicks lived on the opposite side of Walsham le Willows and was digging in the garden when they arrived, planting onion sets. He washed his hands and sat down with them in the kitchen. He was in his late twenties, had a mop of tousled red hair and freckled fair skin and was a bit nervous. He fiddled with his hands whilst Webb explained why they were there. His girlfriend Nancy walked in when she heard voices but excused herself when they said they were there to talk to Paul. "Back to my studies," she sighed, rolling her eyes.

Paul seemed surprised when they told him Archie was dead but didn't seem overly concerned. "I probably knew more about him than he knew about me," he said. "He was a couple of years behind me at the local Comprehensive, so I was aware of him but didn't mix with him then. You tend to keep within your age group, don't you? Anyway, we sometimes go to the Blue Boar in the village. There's a chap Billy there who I'm friendly with; he was in the same year as him at school.

He told me that after I left to work in the drawing office, Archie and another two lads were nearly expelled. They'd often played practical jokes and messed around, possibly to try and impress the girls. They had been caught a couple of times and punished. Anyway, one day, they went one better. They got hold of a bike owned by an unpopular maths teacher called Ferris. Inevitably, it was known as Ferris Wheels. They somehow managed to get it onto the flat roof of the gym, where everyone could see it. They were found out and in trouble for moving the bike and climbing onto the roof. Archie's dad went up to the school, made a lot of fuss, and saved him and the others from getting expelled. They got other punishments instead for a month or so. Billy reckons he also failed most of his exams, but his dad already had a job lined up for him."

"You must have travelled home a similar route on Thursday night. Was Archie still there when you left?" queried Webb.

"Yes, he was talking to his mate Neville Rands when I left, trying to show him some step or other."

"If it was an accident, and I didn't see it, why all the questions?" asked Paul.

"Unfortunately, we believe that his car had been tampered with. Did you see anyone near it then or earlier?" asked Ron.

"Blimey, so it wasn't a real accident then?" responded Paul incredulously. "No, I didn't see anyone. Several of us were leaving at the same time, so I would not have necessarily noticed if someone was next to a car that wasn't theirs. It was dark by then."

"Did you see much of him, living in the same village?" continued Ron.

"Not really. I have been living with Nancy for three years now, and she is studying full-time for a degree in architecture, so we don't have too much cash to splash around. Apart from my Morris, we usually have one visit to the Blue Boar each week. I think Archie generally uses the Six Bells. He did come into the Blue Boar one night a week or so ago with his latest girlfriend for a pub meal. They weren't serving meals at the Six Bells at the time. He said hello and introduced her when they came in. She was quite attractive. Mind you, he seems to have had several different girlfriends since I've known him. Maybe it was one of his ex-girlfriends who fixed his car? You do hear of such things. Well, at least on the TV."

"Do you know the name or address of the girlfriend, please? We would obviously like to speak with her," asked Peggy, pen in hand.

"No, but Nancy does. She knew her slightly. Nancy!" Paul called. After a minute or so, she came down the stairs, looking annoyed at being disturbed.

"Sorry to disturb your essay, love, but who was that girl that Archie brought into the Blue Boar the other week? These policemen would like to know."

"Her name is Amanda Delafond, but she is usually known as Mandy. I don't know the house number, but it is the one that is two doors up from Rolfes Butchers on the Street.

"We'll find it, thank you, and sorry to have disturbed you," apologised Peggy.

"Nancy, Archie was killed in his motor last Thursday night. They think it may have been sabotaged!" exclaimed Paul.

"I don't know him very well, officers, but my guess would be a jealous girlfriend or even a jealous husband!" was Nancy's parting comment.

"One last thing before I let you return to your gardening, please, Mr Hicks," asked Ron. "How did you feel about some of the suggested changes within Woolpit Morris?"

"Mixed feelings, really. It was a friendly side under old Bob, but he ruled it completely. The new Squire seems to be trying to suit everyone but is pleasing no one. I take the role of The Fool, so I am expected to be a good enough dancer to act about and hit people with my bladder on a stick without spoiling the dance. I also do a solo jig. Some older dancers aren't quite as agile as they once were, and their lines may not end completely straight and coordinated. Some of the young ones are ambitious but know that they need a high standard of dancing to be invited to festivals and the like. Mind you, some of them still have a lot to learn about technique. I morris dance because I enjoy it, and it has always been a friendly side. For instance, one lady called Marlene Cooper comes with her husband when we dance out. She brings a tambourine but doesn't always keep time very well. Some stricter sides would tell her to stop, but instead, we have a little private joke about it. If a dancer mucks up a step, we say he is dancing to 'Marlene Time.'

So long as I can enjoy it, I don't mind where I do it, locally or nationally, but I don't want arguments about what should be a pleasant hobby. I can get enough of those at work, thank you!"

"Yes, I can understand that", sympathised Ron (not free of arguments at his work either, thanks to His Lordship). "Well, thank you and goodbye."

Morris Murder

Chapter 7

Saturday, 11th March, 2017

Inevitably, Webb and Catchpole sought out the girlfriend, Mandy Delafond, next and quickly found the home from the directions. Her mother opened the door and invited the pair in. The sound of loud music could be heard from upstairs. "I will just go up and get her. She'll never hear me shout with that din!" she said, going upstairs. There was a pause, and the music shut off abruptly, and Mandy came down. After introductions, she invited them to sit in the lounge and noticeably addressed her comments to Peggy. Mandy had blonde hair piled upon her head, cupid bow lips and a clear complexion. She curled her legs around beneath her on her armchair and withdrew her hands into the overlong sleeves of a baggy green sweater. Ron slightly nodded to Peggy, indicating that she should lead the questioning.

"I believe that you know Archie Berry," opened Peggy tentatively.

"I've been out with him a couple of times, but it is over. I dumped him last Wednesday night."

"Would you mind telling me why?"

"Well, I had been out with him once before, and we'd gone out to the Blue Boar in the village for a bite. He'd been trying to chat me up for ages, and I suppose I finally gave in. Anyway, he was very attentive and polite and gave me a couple of compliments. He walked me home, and we kissed on the doorstep. He called me the next day and asked to go out with me again. We swapped texts a few times, and then he took me to a restaurant in Bury St Edmunds last Wednesday night after work. We sat there chatting when another couple came in and sat at a table behind me, off to one side. The bloke had his back to us, and his date was facing my back. She was quite pretty, I suppose, but a bit obvious, if you know what I mean. Half a yard of thigh showing, and her boobs nearly jumping out of her neckline. Ugh!

I realised that Archie was ogling her and only half listening to what I was saying. This went on for a bit until I was fed up. I said, "I was considering splitting the bill with you tonight, but you'd better split it with the one you have been spending the most attention on!" Then I got up and left. Do you know he never even tried to come after me? I had to get a cab back from Bury."

"How awful!" commiserated Peggy. "I think I would have done the same, so well done you. Have you seen him since?

"No, and I don't want to, whatever excuse he comes up with."

"Well, that will not arise. Unfortunately, he was killed in a car crash the following night," explained Peggy calmly.

"Oh no! How horrible. That could have me in there with him if we hadn't split up. Where did it happen?"

"Just outside Woolpit. No offence, I have to ask everyone about this sort of thing. Where were you on Thursday night between 8 and 10?"

"You think I might have done it? No, I might have felt like killing him on Wednesday night, but like they say on the soaps, 'he's not worth it!' My friend Gill came around and did my nails. You can ask her." She ferreted out a business card, handed it over, and pushed her hands out from her cuffs to display ten polished pink digits.

"Another one bites the dust", commented Webb when they got back into the car. "But check out her alibi with the beautician just for safety's sake, please. I think that is enough for today. My tummy is rumbling! Let's divide up the rest of the Morris men between us tomorrow. It works out to about five each. We may not find out anything else about them, but it seems likely that the sabotage happened in that village hall car park whilst they were practising. Whether it was one of them or somebody else who knew Archie's movements, who knows at this stage? As that

Morris Murder

lass Nancy suggested, it could even be a disgruntled ex-girlfriend."

"Hell hath no fury like a woman scorned and all that. Yes, it is possible," concluded Catchpole. "I'll drive over in my car tomorrow then. Let me take down the details of the ones you want me to cover. We stand a better chance of catching them at home on a Sunday."

"Yes, good. Don't forget to keep a note of your hours this weekend. I know you weren't rostered to work, so thanks for helping me. It's up to you if you take it as overtime or T.O.I.L., but I see you have built up a fair backlog of that. I don't want you disappearing for a month!"[5]

"Darn it, there goes that extended Caribbean Cruise then!" Peggy joked. "Would you like me to take the musicians? There are some ladies amongst them."

"Yes, please, that will be excellent," confirmed Ron.

---

[5] Sergeants and Constables can choose to take Time Off In Lieu (TOIL) or be paid for extra hours worked. Inspectors and above do not get paid for any overtime.

Chapter 8

Sunday, 12th March, 2017

Peggy headed for Elmswell first on Sunday to the home of Julie Canning, the fiddler. She passed an ancient church and some almshouses before reaching the village and past the closed-down bacon factory that had once been a significant employer. It turned out that Julie lived with her parents close to the railway crossing of one of the few railway stations in the area. Julie was tall, slim, and had long auburn hair woven into a plaited pigtail. She was dressed neatly to go to church with her parents but told them to go on without her. "I only go to please them!" she whispered when they had gone. She was a bit reticent to talk at first, but once she had got over the shock of hearing about Archie's death, she opened up. She told Peggy that she was 21 and worked as a dental nurse in Stowmarket.

"I got quite friendly with Archie before last summer," she said, looking wistful. "Then, in August, we bumped into each other at the Folkeast festival at Little Glemham. It is up towards Lowestoft and is quite large. I was supposed to be going with Elspeth from Woolpit Morris, but she got sick at the last minute, so I camped alone. I wasn't going to miss Blowzabella, Eliza Carthy and John Spiers! Sorry, I should explain, they are big folk stars. To cut an embarrassing long story short, Archie spent the nights in my tent." She looked over at Peggy, who showed no adverse reaction, so she carried on. "I was hoping that things would continue after the festival, but apart from a single text, they didn't. I got the feeling that he avoids commitment: I have heard that there have been several girls since then, none of whom have lasted very long. Maybe he is just after conquests? I don't know, but it has made things a little awkward. We speak, but only pleasantries.

The awful thing is, I realised when you told me just now that I had passed that accident going home that night. I didn't know it was him until just now. Emergency services were there, and I'm not particularly eager to look. I just got past it and came home. I was later than Archie because we had been discussing a tune at the end, and Billy (the melodeon player) asked whether we would like to do a barn dance booking in Wetherden with him. We sometimes go out together as a band, with Peter Mottram acting as the caller for dancers. I guess I had come to class Archie as a 'might have been', but it was sad for him to have died so young."

Nothing more was said, so Peggy continued to Pakenham, where Elspeth Charles lived. The village prides itself on having the only working watermill in Suffolk, a windmill, a pub, a church and a Post Office, and plenty of social activities go on there. Elspeth lived alone in a small cottage and had a heap of homework she was marking on the kitchen table when Peggy arrived. "I could do with a break from this!" she said. "Julie was just on the phone, so I know why you are here. Let me put the kettle on, then I will be with you. I should give up trying to teach my students any semblance of spelling or grammar."

"That bad, huh?" sympathised Peggy. "Gone are the days of criminals writing their statements. If we didn't accept dictation, the courts would never be able to read them!"

"I gather that Julie passed the accident without realising who it was. He left a bit before us because we discussed some stuff at the end. I play Melodeon and learn quite a bit from Billy Newson. I'm actually the granddaughter of Bob Spurgeon, who was Squire until recently. My dad got me into Woolpit Morris when I was younger, and I am four years older than her. Dad had to drop out dancing because of a bad knee injury." She paused to make them mugs of tea.

"So, being in the group for a while, I guess you would know most of the dancers and their squabbles?" prompted Peggy.

"As musicians, we certainly get to observe them more, but I know some better than others. I wouldn't mind going off to a festival or two during the summer holidays from school, but I guess that is not for everyone. They expect a high standard of dancing if you get booked for that sort of thing, and some of the more senior dancers are not as spry as they once were.

You probably heard that Archie was keen to make changes but didn't get enough support from the others. Don't repeat it, but we have such a useless new Squire. I know that I am probably biased, but he isn't half the man my Grandad was. If you know what I mean, he is too nice and sits on the fence too much, which will not do. Mind you, I cannot imagine any dancer getting so angry as to damage Archie's car. It is more likely to be some upset girlfriend, although not Julie. I hasten to add she is too timid. I know what happened between Julie and Archie. She told me long ago, but it was apparent that she was pretty doe-eyed about him then. I never told her I had a fling with him before she joined the side. It was never that serious, and I didn't expect it to be. I have never told her because I think it would upset her, feeling she was second choice."

DS Catchpole couldn't quite figure out why the fact may upset Julie but let it pass. It seemed that Elspeth had no real connection to Archie nowadays and had a more cavalier approach to her liaison with him, which was the important thing. She'd got a new angle on what passed for

Morris' gossip. It also corroborated Julie's account of last Thursday evening.

"With Archie dumping Julie, were there others who may have felt bad on her behalf?" Peggy queried.

"I don't think that anyone else knew. It was quite discreet, but no doubt others would like to get to know her better. Peter Mottram, our barn dance caller, obviously fancies her, but she isn't interested in him. I'm sure he'd like a mixed dance side to give him more opportunities to meet ladies, but I don't think that will happen any time soon. I suppose he is alright, but he is a bit of an oddball, even by our eccentric standards. Don't get him talking about clocks if you see him – he will lecture you for hours, given half the chance."

Peggy took that as her cue. "Yes, I also have to go there, so thank you for the warning. I'd better get on, but thanks for the tea and information. Both are well appreciated."

Peggy drove up the road and got out her notebook. She hadn't managed to get everything Elspeth said down, so she made some quick notes before she forgot. Then she opened her sandwich box, which she had prepared last night before going to bed, and thoughtfully picked at a salad with grated cheese on it with a plastic fork.

Then, checking her directions, she started the engine again and headed for Great Barton. The Bunbury Arms seemed to be doing a good trade for its Sunday Roast, advertised on a board outside, with the car park full. Peggy regretfully thought she would have preferred that to the salad but promised herself a take-away Chinese meal on the way home.

Billy Newson had a sign outside his house announcing that he was a furniture upholsterer, repairer and French polisher. On telling him why she was there, he called for his wife Shirley in a broad Suffolk accent and insisted that she repeat it all to her. "Just as well," she commented. "He doesn't remember anything unless it is written down. Fifty going on eighty," she exclaimed, and Billy laughed and took no offence.

"It's true. I have a repertoire of about fifty dance tunes I can remember, but ask me what I had for dinner last night, and I will have forgotten."

"You have never forgotten to turn up for a meal in your life, though, have you, Billy Newson?" his wife laughed, pointing at the rotund belly beneath his plaid shirt. "And in case you ask, it was Shepherd's Pie, and we are having the other half today. I can't get used to cooking for two since our kids left home and married," she confided.

"What can you remember about Archie then, Mr Newson," DS Catchpole asked.

"Lads like him are the future of Woolpit Morris, not the old fogeys!" he declared. "Old gits like me should make way for the next generation before we become a joke. I'm training up another couple of musicians who will eventually be able to take over from me. Fine young Mawthers they are![6] The side still needs me now, and I enjoy it, so no problem. My Shirley is in the Haughley Hoofers, you know. They are a smashing ladies' dance group. They do Northwest Clog, which is very different, don't you love?" Shirley nodded.

"So, can you think of anyone who might have grudge enough to sabotage Archie's car then?" asked Peggy, trying to bring the interview back on track.

"Naw, that doesn't figure at all," was the reply. "Thus a wholly fair bunch of bohrs."[7]

It was fortunate that Peggy grew up in Suffolk. A London detective may have thought that Billy was talking in some local criminal code. She decided to say her farewell in the way she had

---

[6] Mawther, Suffolk dialect for young women, and not a corruption of 'mother.'

[7] Doesn't figure – doesn't make sense. Wholly fair – good   Bohrs – men and boys Suffolk Dialect

learned as a child. "Well, I've best be going-on. Fare thee well, tigither."

Royston Nichols of Stowlangtoft was much less forthcoming. Peggy guessed he was in his late fifties and had a prominent nose and ruddy face. His head penetrated his hair like a monk's tonsure, and Royston had liver spots on his bare arms. He proudly pointed to the colourful Oss structure sitting on a cupboard in the corner of the hall. It imitated a horse with a head, mane, reins and tail and was to be suspended from the shoulders by a pair of broad straps. The body was designed to go around the dancer like a bizarre sort of life belt. Small-booted legs hung at the sides, in denial of the longer legs of the dancer protruding from the bottom of the body. His wife, Rosemary, a sour-faced woman, snorted in disgust. "Blinking old thing spoils the look of the place. He comes back from dancing worn out, red in the face and wheezing. It's about time he gave it up, the old fool!" She stomped off in high dudgeon.

The old fool in question grinned and shook his head. "She has never liked Morris, but it is the one thing that gets me out of the house now that I am semi-retired. I'm a painter and decorator, but I have to choose which jobs I can manage nowadays. Now, how can I help you, my dear?"

Peggy repeated the story for the umpteenth time and watched as his wrinkled face crumpled. "Oh no! That's terrible! He was a nice young chap. I didn't always agree with him, but he was keen and a good dancer. What a waste! His poor parents, losing one so young." Royston was clearly upset at what he had just heard. It was challenging to fake his expression, thought Peggy, experienced at hearing whole catalogues of lies from suspects. She continued asking whether he had spotted anyone doing anything unusual in the car park and learnt that he had a lift with 'Ducky' from Langham and had seen nothing of note. She left soon after to seek out her final interview of the day at Wetherden. "Of course," she mused in the car, "a decorator would possess a large pair of wallpaper scissors but would be unlikely to take them with him when given a lift."

Wetherden has a well-used village hall and one pub called the Maypole, but no longer has any shops or a post office. Curiously, the village pump is under shelter, as if they feared the water getting wet. In this rural idyll lives Peter Mottram, a 26-year-old clock repairer. After introducing herself on the step of his old cottage on the main street, Peggy had to pick her way through the remains of many defunct clocks, magnifying lights, boxes of cogs and springs and mysterious-looking tools that had turned his front room into a workshop. In the back kitchen, they sat on the only two upright chairs on either side of a small table covered with oilcloth. Peter had an intense stare, probably gained from his work looking at the tiny clock and watch movements, but it was matched with an almost staccato voice. He seemed to chatter a sentence, pause for thought, then set off again. Maybe it resulted from him living alone for twelve years since his father died, Peggy thought. She explained why she was there.

"Goodness!" he exclaimed. "That someone could engineer a death in such a way, but cars are such crude pieces of machinery compared with clocks."

Forewarned, Peggy headed him off from the subject of all things horological. "Did you spot anything unusual in the carpark?" she asked hurriedly.

"No, but it was dark when we came out. They ought to put up a light there. They could have it on a sensor so that it wasn't burning electricity all the time," he mused, seemingly delighted at his suggestion and oblivious to the crime.

"Can you think of anyone who might have had a grudge against Archie?" Peggy persisted. He paused to think.

Morris Murder

"No, I doubt that it would be anyone from the Morris. Or Woolpit: it is such a lovely place. I should look for an outsider if I were you."

"I understand that you act as a barn dance caller. That must be fun," ventured Peggy, putting away her notebook and preparing to leave.

"Oh yes, seeing people dancing with each other is lovely. You don't have to come with a partner or know the dances beforehand. Half the fun is getting it wrong! You must come to one. You would be very welcome!"

Peggy escaped and was glad to get back to her car. She wasn't really frightened of Peter Mottram, but he was a bit un-nerving in his manner. She was happy to head home.

Morris Murder

Chapter 9

Sunday, 12th March, 2017

Ron thought he should have been starting to prune his precious roses today instead of heading for Rougham. He was familiar with the industrial estate that had grown up around the old wartime airfield and control tower. It could be glimpsed from the A14, but he had never driven into the village before.

The home of Robin 'Robbo' Cooper and his wife Tina was near a primary school, and they invited them into their front room. It seemed oddly dated. He estimated that they were in their mid-forties, but the brown three-piece suite appeared to be from the early fifties, and there was a flight of three plaster geese on the wall above where he was sitting. Maybe the house and its furnishings were inherited. Robbo was very tall and dwarfed his much shorter wife. He had a prominent Adam's apple and a straggly, overgrown moustache that complemented a pair of sagging, sad eyes. She was a complete contrast, bubbly and cheery in every way, bustling about with nervous energy.

Ron explained why he was visiting. The couple seemed shocked, and while they expressed their horror, Ron noticed some photos on the opposite wall of banger racing cars with their mechanics and drivers.

Morris Murder

"Is that you in those pictures?" he inquired.

"Oh yes, from when I was much younger. I used to help my Dad prepare and repair the banger racing cars. We used to travel to the circuits at Foxhall, near Ipswich and so on. It was great fun, but I gave it up when we married and moved."

"This is my childhood home," explained Tina. "We lived here with my Mother until she died last year. I'm still not over it, but we have fun in the summer with the morris. I usually go along to and bang a tambourine."

"That works out well," commented Robbo. "Tina doesn't drink, so she drives, and I can have a pint or two."

"We enjoy the social side and getting together in the pub afterwards. They often get him to sing a folk song or two. He's got a lovely voice," added Tina.

"Yes, it makes a break from working all the time. I drive a delivery lorry for Thomas Ridley, the local food wholesaler. I have been there for over 20 years now. That Archie worked at a garden centre, didn't he?"

"Yes, he did," confirmed Ron. "Did you see anyone lurking around his motor last Thursday night, or do you know anyone that might want to hurt him?" questioned Ron.

Morris Murder

"No, nothing like that," replied Robbo. "I mean, some of us older ones didn't agree with his ideas for the morris, but not so we'd ever hurt him. I must admit, although he was a good dancer, we didn't particularly warm to him ourselves, did we, Tina?"

"No, we like Woolpit Morris the way it is. Why can't they all just get on with one another?" she railed. "Then there was another thing: I wanted to sell my jam and marmalade into the garden centre, but Archie said they needed proper barcode labels, sell-by dates and trackability. I couldn't be doing with all that malarkey! Still, I work as a part-time receptionist at the doctor, and he doesn't mind me having a little table to sell some to the patients."

Ron left the Coopers thinking about the banger racing pictures. Robbo obviously knew his way around motors, and the couple didn't seem particularly enamoured with Archie. He fortified himself with another humbug and carried on to Norton. A mix of houses was set back from either side of the main road, and there was a combined shop and petrol station.

Roger Causton was in his mid-thirties and was just about to walk to the Norton Dog for a drink when Ron called. He had a tweed jacket, flat cap, khaki pullover and brown trousers. His face was pink, flushed, and dominated by an oversized pair of Harry Potter spectacles. There were many boxes of books lined up against the wall, awaiting the provision of some bookshelves by the looks of it.

Roger told Ron that he had moved from Shropshire for a history teaching job at Stowmarket last September. "I was in an ambitious dance side back there, with no knackered 'old guard' like Woolpit. It does get confusing sometimes. I used to dance the 'Young Collins' stick dance and 'Bonnets so Blue' handkerchief from the Bledington village tradition. They do the versions from Bampton here, and they are subtly different, with a change to the stepping. Still, I should be up to speed by the time the season begins on May 1st."

"Not that long to go then," commented Webb. "Do you think the death of Archie will affect the side?"

"Inevitably," replied Causton confidently. "He was the mouthpiece for the young Turks who wanted to see some progress. I suppose we will be stuck with the old codgers for a bit longer. It is a sad shame about Archie. He had a spark of life to him. Mind you, I wouldn't think that any of the old guard would have the gumption to try and get rid of him. They don't like any change, you probably know."

As Webb left, he reflected that Causton appeared very pro-Archie and the proposed changes. Was this to deflect attention from himself? Why should a teacher in their mid-thirties move all the way from Shropshire for another job? It didn't seem to be a promotion, something he might have been expecting to go for at his age. Sitting in his car and making some notes, he ate the corned beef sandwiches Alice had packed for him and bit into an apple while checking the map directions for Langham. He had a sat-nav but liked to fix in his mind where places actually were in relation to each other.

Langham has no shop, pub or village hall, and the church is separate from the village in a field with no direct road leading to it. The hamlet is home to no more than about 100 people, so it wasn't tricky for Webb to find the home of Dougal 'Ducky' Dransfield. His wife Ann answered the door and let him in. He looked up from the television but didn't turn it off, so she did. Webb estimated them to be in their mid-twenties. The room was cold, and Ann had a thick hand-knitted jumper over some leggings. Dougal didn't seem to feel the cold and sat in a polo shirt and jeans.

Once again, Webb repeated his story. "You must have come home the same way," said Ann.

"Yes, probably," Dougal answered with a growl, giving her a dark look. "But I didn't see anything. I left the hall sharpish. I wanted to get to bed quickly. I was on an early shift in Stowmarket the next morning."

"What do you do there?" enquired Ron pleasantly.

"I'm a forklift driver for Baxter & Hall."

"Did you see anything suspicious in the carpark around Archie's car at all?"

"No. Can't say I was looking," was the retort. There was a slightly awkward silence, broken by Ann.

"I dance in Haughley Hoofers, but fortunately, we practice on different nights so the other one can look after the baby." Realising that there was no sign of an infant, she added, "She is asleep upstairs. Kept me up most of the night, the little devil."

Webb smiled, but it wasn't terribly genuine. Dougal was clearly unfriendly to policemen from his attitude, and so he left. As he got back into his car, he realised that he hadn't asked about what Dougal thought of Archie and his ideas but decided to leave it for now. Dougal Dransfield was young, so he may be amenable to going further away to dance, but a baby and a wife who danced with another group may get in the way. Sighing, he looked up the details of the last person to interview today, who lived in Tostock, a village spread out over a wide area.

Webb passed The Gardner's Arms pub, St Andrews Church and a village hall before he found the home of Alan 'Wilky' Wilkinson. According to Harry Scrivener, he had not been present last Thursday night, but that did not excuse him from being a suspect in Ron's mind. He reasoned that he could have entered the car park without entering the hall.

Alan opened the door and took the time to examine Webb's warrant card before letting him into his flat. It was the ground floor of a house that had been divided into two. The room was untidy, with discarded fast-food boxes and clothes lying around. Alan himself looked tired and dishevelled as if he had just woken up. He rubbed his eyes several times and yawned.

"I understand that you have to miss some of the practice sessions for Woolpit Morris because of working shifts, Mr Wilkinson," Ron said by way of opening.

"Yes, that's right. I work at the Port of Ipswich, so I cannot always make it," he explained.

"Last Thursday night, Archie Berry left the practice and crashed on the way home. I'm sorry to say that he was killed. There is a possibility that his car had been tampered with."

"Blimey, that's a shock. I wasn't there, and I hadn't heard."

"I understand that there had been some disagreements within the group since the old Squire had to retire. What is your take on that?" asked Webb.

"Well, Bob Spurgeon had helped found Woolpit Morris with me and some other dancers from Hageneth. He had been the leader ever since and ensured things were done his way. That suited me because I agreed with him most of the time. I might well have succeeded him, but they voted for Harry Scrivener instead. He is a lovely man, but some of the younger members have been taking the opportunity to suggest some changes.

I think Archie was probably the ringleader of that, but I don't blame him. He is young and ambitious and likely split the vote. I'm not trying to be rude because I regard him as a friend, but I think Harry was seen as an easier touch than me to agree to changes. The trouble is, I don't think he is a strong enough leader to keep things together, and he tries to keep everybody happy, which doesn't always work. I reckon the younger elements might have broken away and formed their own side, which would be a pity. Whether that would happen now that Archie is gone is probably more doubtful.

"So, you weren't keen on Archie and his plans?" asked Ron, trying to clarify all the information he had been given.

"No, I wasn't. I guess part of it is personal as well. I can confidentially tell you that I have always fancied one of the lady musicians, called Julie, but he beat me to it there. I don't think the others knew, but they were an item for a short while, but he dumped her. After that, she was off dating all Morris men, including me."

DCI Webb thanked him and headed for home. Despite seeming honest about his feelings towards Archie, Ron still made a note to get someone to check out his alibi for last Thursday night.

Morris Murder

Chapter 10

Monday, 13th March, 2017

All of the team were at work early on Monday morning, eager to hear what progress had been made by the others over the weekend and share the information they had obtained themselves. DCI Webb chaired the room whilst DS Catchpole added new points to the crowded whiteboard. She had already listed all Woolpit Morris members on the left-hand side.

"DS Catchpole and I have interviewed all of the members of Woolpit Morris over the weekend," announced Webb. The pair went on to add comments about each of the names. Also added to the board were headings entitled 'Parents', 'Girlfriends' and 'Work Colleagues.' "We shall visit the garden centre later today, where Archie worked, to see if they can shed any light on the matter," concluded Ron. Just then, the door opened, and a stranger entered, accompanied by someone from reception.

"Good Morning," the smartly suited stranger said. "I really must apologise profusely for breaking into your meeting. I know how vital they are and wouldn't do this unless necessary. DCI Webb, could you spare me a couple of minutes in the privacy of your office, please?"

Ron paused and then said, "DS Catchpole will continue running this briefing. I will be back as soon as possible." He tried to remain calm and professional but was inwardly seething. The officer had better have an excellent reason. He did.

"Sorry, but I had no choice. I am Inspector Sharp from the Met, acting on behalf of the Independent Police Complaints Commission. I have to arrest and question your DC, Jim Corcoran. Is he present this morning?"

"Yes, he is the curly-haired young man sitting at the front over there," answered Webb with some credulity. "You chaps don't get involved unless there is a grave complaint. What on earth is he supposed to have done?"

"Sorry, but I cannot tell you that yet. It relates to an alleged incident involving a member of the public when he was still in uniform. He is allowed to have a Police Federation rep. or colleague present as 'Policeman's Friend."

"Well, I don't know what he is supposed to have done, but he has been an excellent officer here. I picked him myself last year to be seconded after seeing him in action, and I have not regretted it yet," stated Ron. "You had better go and sort yourself an interview room out and maybe get a coffee. I'm sure the receptionist there will help you. I will call him in here with my DS and send him through."

Inspector Sharp left, and Ron paused momentarily before quietly summoning Corcoran and Catchpole. "Shut the door. I have some bad news," he said solemnly, explaining what was happening. Of course, Jim was shocked and said he had no idea what it was about. "If it were an ordinary police behavioural complaint, it would be investigated by our own Suffolk Police Professional Standards Department. All I can tell you is that it is from when you were in uniform and relates to a complaint from a member of the public, which is why IPCC is involved." Jim shook his head in disbelief and looked close to tears. "You have been an excellent officer here, and I told him so. I wish you the best of luck," added Webb. "Keep your chin up!"

"Would you accompany me, Sarge, please?" Jim asked in a shaky voice. "I would rather have somebody with me that I know and who knows me."

"Of course," said Peggy. "But you must understand that I will simply be there to ensure you have a fair interview and a chance to speak for yourself. I cannot advise on law or what to say or do, but to stick to the questions asked and tell the truth. You will be under the same caution as any other suspect." Jim nodded, and Peggy

Morris Murder

led the way to the suite of interview rooms. The rest of the team were agog but did not say anything as they passed through but guessed that something serious was afoot. DCI Webb returned to speak to them before they could get into discussion and speculation.

"Attention! As you have no doubt gathered, something is going on. I cannot speak to you about it at present, but I will let you know when I know something. It has nothing to do with our case. I want you to focus on finding Archie's killer. You will keep what you know within this room. We have a ton of information but no real leads. Those people we have spoken to and have any doubts about will get a tick by their names here on the board, and we will endeavour to check their stories out. DC Cateby, I would like you to accompany me to the Garden Centre. DC Winter, please check whether Alan Wilkinson was at work last Thursday night. If you can, see if you can dig up why Roger Causton might have made a sideways move from Shropshire. We are now two officers down, so please do as much as possible and follow up on any leads."

Chapter 11

Monday, 13th March, 2017

DC Will Cateby was pleased to go to the garden centre with his boss. He had put on a tie and jacket when he found that he was going out on official business. He tended to get stuck with office-based work often and didn't want to be known just for delving into suspects' bank accounts and social media, practical though it was. "Take notes of what they say and keep an eye on their body language," instructed Ron, offering him the inevitable humbug. "If there is something relevant that you think is not being explored, don't be afraid to chip in. I don't mind that – two heads are better than one."

Badwell Ash Garden Centre and Nursery was a medium-sized business on the outskirts of the village. There were only a handful of cars parked when they arrived, and they soon found the owner, Jimmy Allsop. When they introduced themselves, he ushered them into the small office away from any customers. It was neat and well-ordered, and Jimmy sat on the corner of the desktop so that they could occupy the only two chairs. He was grey-haired and weatherbeaten, with a green company fleece over his white shirt and three-quarter-length cargo pants.

"This is usually Cecil Berry's office," he stated. "He rang me on Friday and told me what had

Morris Murder

happened, so I gave him some time off. He is my general manager here and is very reliable. I am semi-retired now, but I have come in to cover for the absences. Archie oversaw the shop side of things for us. He was a nice chap, got on well with the customers, and was learning the trade well. I'd hoped he would mature like his father here. I try to recruit locally. Then staff are more loyal and can get here when the roads are rough. Of course, Archie travelled with his Dad most days. How can I be of help?"

"We believe that Archie's car may have been sabotaged. Is there anyone here who may have had a grudge against him?" asked Ron.

"Gracious, no! So, you think it may not have been an accident? Poor Cecil and his wife, Avril. It must be heartbreaking for them. As for anyone not liking him, I'm unaware of any problems, but feel free to talk to them all. They all know that Archie died. Angela, Nicky, and Simone are in the centre, and Manny is out in the greenhouses. I will leave you to wander about by yourselves because I must cover the shop and take in some deliveries. Come back to me if there is anything you need."

"Thank you, Mr Allsop," said Ron. "Just one last thing that I have to ask everybody. Can you please tell me your whereabouts between 8-10 pm last Thursday night?"

Morris Murder

"Oh, no problem. I know it is part of your job. I was at a Masonic dinner in Ipswich. A couple of your colleagues were there and should be able to vouch for me. Do you know Alex Hardy?"

"I do indeed, sir. Thank you very much." As Allsop left them to attend to a customer, Cateby half-whispered, "Is that His Lordship, sir?"

"Yes, all we need is a friend of the governer. He will stick his oar in if he knows a fellow Brother is involved." He led Cateby towards the café attached to the business. "Fancy a coffee? We have to start somewhere, so let's talk to the lass in there." They were the only customers at this time of the morning. Having ordered a Latte for himself and a Cappuccino for Cateby, Webb introduced himself to the lady with 'Simone Arnold, Catering Manager' on her name badge. She wore a caterers mob cap over her short, brown hair and an apron over her company fleece. Her face had a world-weary look, which had a hint of eye shadow but no other make-up.

"I suppose you are here about Archie? Mr Allsop told us about the accident on Friday, and his Dad has been given a couple of days off," she informed them.

"Yes, so I understand. I suppose you must have known him well in a small company like this?" Ron ventured.

95

Morris Murder

"Not as well as he would have liked," Simone sneered. "He thought he was God's gift to Women, Business, the lot. Archie wasn't! He tried to be flirty with me, and I soon told him where to go! I've got a man. Why should I want a boy?"

"Fair enough," commented Ron. "I have to ask everyone, can you tell me where you were last Thursday evening, please? It's just a formality."

"I expect at home with my boyfriend watching TV," Simone answered casually. "Yes, that's the night 'Last Kingdom' was on. We both like that."

"Thank you very much. Can you please direct me to the toilet?" added Ron. She pointed the way, and Webb left Cateby there, finishing his coffee.

"Fancied himself a bit, did he?" Cateby asked conversationally, putting his notebook away.

Simone leaned over her counter. "He wouldn't even have had a job here if his Dad hadn't pulled a few strings. Nice to have a Dad who's the boss, eh? Just as his son left school, he got rid of the old shop boss!"

"What was the old manager's name? Would I know him?" asked DC Cateby in feigned innocence.

"No, I heard he died a year or two back. What was his name now? Oh, I know. Benny. I don't think I ever knew his last name. He was Benny to everyone," she recalled. Just then, Webb returned from the loo, and they searched for the other staff members. A young female assistant was filling up a shelf with bottles of plant food. She seemed pretty engrossed in her task and didn't notice them at first. She had cropped brown hair, powerful specs and a slightly spotty complexion.

"Good morning, we are from the police. May I ask your name, please?" asked Ron pleasantly.

"I'm Angela Swann. Can I help you?"

"I hope so. We are trying to find out a bit about Archie Berry. I presume you worked with him?"

"Oh yeah. He wasn't too bad as a boss. That's a shame about his accident. They told us on Friday."

"What was he like?" asked Ron, gently.

"To be honest, a bit weird and geeky. He was always on about Morris dancing. All that waving hankies about, you know. It's a bit odd, isn't it?"

"I suppose so," agreed Ron. "I have to ask everyone, what were you up to last Thursday night?"

"Nothing! Why the questions? I was in the White Horse until about half-past nine, then my friend and I got some chips at Rumbles."

"You still have a chip shop in the village? Excellent, that's our lunch sorted out today then," laughed Ron, evading her question. "Cheerio then, I'll just catch your colleague as well while I am here," he continued, moving off sharply towards another young female assistant pulling a trolley load of potted plants. Cateby followed in his wake.

After introducing himself, he interviewed Nicky Everton, who was very forthcoming. "I work in the shop, the Café and the greenhouse, wherever I'm most needed. I didn't like him much and didn't have too much to do with him if I could help it. I just did what he said and got on with it."

"Why was that?" enquired Ron.

"He ogled all the women and looked at my boobs instead of my face too often, if you must know. The creepy perv! I'm not bothered that he has gone at all!" she said, with disgust on her face. It has to be admitted, thought Ron to himself, that she does have an ample bosom beneath her fleece and a pretty face. Returning from his reverie, he asked, "Can you tell me where you were last Thursday night, please?"

"What, you think I might have done it? Give me a break! I've better things to do on a Thursday night. I help run the local Brownie pack at St Mary's Church. A couple of dozen little darlings and their mothers saw me there. Mind you, I suppose I could have sent the pack out to get their Assassins Badge. I'm awful, aren't I? But that's how I deal with things."

"That just leaves the chap in the greenhouse," said Webb as they walked away. He paused to look at some rose plants wistfully. "No, I mustn't buy any more," he said half to himself. "There is no more room, and Alice would moan." He commented to his colleague, "Funny that the other young lass, Angela, didn't complain about Archie being a letch."

"Well, I'm trying not to be judgemental here, sir, but Angela was flat-chested and quite plain, whilst Nicky is more attractive to my mind," responded Cateby.

"Yes, that's true, I suppose. I suppose there is no harm in appreciating life's finer things. Are you still going out with that Gloria?" Ron asked.

"Oh yes, sir, it's been over six months now. We are planning to go on holiday together in Spain. She's 'the one'," admitted Will, surprised that his boss remembered his girlfriend.

"Good for you. Now, where are the greenhouses?"

"Out of this door and around the side to the left, I believe," informed Will, returning to a safer topic.

Manny Fyfield, the Plants manager, was an older gentleman who puffed a pipe while he tended some plants. He had a flat cap and the same green woollen fleece as all the other employees over a pair of jeans.

"Oh yes, I was told about Archie last Friday. Bad business to die like that," Manny commented. "When he worked here in the greenhouse after school, he had no idea about plants and frequently got it wrong because he didn't listen. I'm glad they put him in charge of the shop and didn't keep him with me. I only get part-time help during the busy season. I can do everything here in winter with some help from young Nicky. Nowadays, I haven't had so much to do with him. When I did, he tried to tell me what sells and what doesn't, but I don't think he really knew."

"I just need to check where everybody was last Thursday night, Mr Fyfield," said Ron.

"I was playing in a darts match over at Stowlangtoft Dark Horse. We beat them good and proper!" Ron thanked him and turned to go,

Morris Murder

but Will Cateby intervened with one last question.

"You've been here a long time, so I wonder if you could answer something that's been troubling me? There used to be a man here in the shop a few years ago. I think his name might have been Benny. Do you remember him?"

"Oh yes, Benny Dransfield. Funny little short fellow. I don't know where he went after leaving here, though."

"Thank you very much," said Will. "That's the name I was trying to remember. Goodbye!"

When they returned to the car, Ron said, "Did you notice how they all wore green company fleeces? I wonder if they are the same colour as the trace on the brake pipes?"

"That's a good thought!" responded Will. "I must admit I hadn't made the connection."

"Never mind, you'll learn," said Webb kindly. "Now, what was that business about the old employee just then? Did you used to come here?"

"No, I've never been here before. I was just about to tell you," said Will. "When you went off to the loo, I kept talking to Simone, the café manager, pretending to gossip casually. "She implied that Mr Berry senior had gotten rid of

101

someone so Archie could get a job here. She could only remember the man's name as Benny."

"So you just got our Mr Fyfield to fill in the gap. So, wait a minute, that makes the bloke –"

"Benny Dransfield!" interrupted Cateby excitedly. "It seems a big coincidence that one of our Morris men also has the same surname. It is not that common as a surname."

"Well done! You are right, and that possible connection is impressive. Now, back to base and follow that lead!"

Elsewhere, Harry Scrivener, the Squire of Woolpit Morris, had said he would not talk to the side until Monday. He put a formal note into their private members' Facebook group:

Woolpit Morris Private Members Facebook Group

Harry: *Hello, everyone. For those who do not already know, I am sorry to tell you that our fellow dancer Archie Berry died in a car crash on the way home from practice last Thursday night. We shall remember him as an excellent dancer, and I have sent a condolence card to his parents. I will let you know the funeral arrangements as soon as they tell me the date. The Police visited and said that there was a possibility that his car had been tampered with.*

Obviously, if anyone saw anything odd in the carpark last Thursday, you have a duty to tell them. I will see you all, hopefully at practice this Thursday. Please be on time.

Robbo: *The police visited me as well. Did they call on everyone?*

Wilky: *Yes, they were asking questions here as well.*

Clacky: *Yeh, the filth was here too. They should have been out looking for the murderer instead of wasting time.*

Paul: *I cannot believe it could be anyone in the side who messed with his car. We have our ups and downs, but this is different.*

Elspeth: *It was only reported as an accident in the newspaper today —no mention of anything else. Have the Police definitely said the car had been fiddled with?*

Nev: *I don't think they said anything about sabotage to me.*

Joolz: *They didn't seem precisely sure, only that it was suspected. The awful thing is, I passed the accident without knowing it was him. All the emergency vehicles blocked the road, and a policeman waved me through.*

Roger: *How terrible. He was a good dancer. We shall miss him.*

Morris Murder

Chapter 12

Monday, 13th March, 2017

Back in the interview room, DC Jim Corcoran was struggling. Inspector Sharp had given him a formal caution and set the evidence tape machine running. DS Catchpole sat at his side, and they faced the interviewer across the table, which was bolted to the floor. The room was hot and airless, and the harsh strip lighting emitted an annoying buzz. Sharp shuffled his papers and paused for effect. Interviewing police officers was a skilled job since they knew many of the techniques used.

"The time period I am interested in was January 2014. I believe you had only recently completed your basic training and were based at Ipswich Police Station. What do you recall about that time there?"

Still mystified about what Sharp was leading up to, Corcoran commented blandly. "I was under Sergeant Knowles. He accompanied me for a week and then put me with various officers on his watch for a week at a time. It was a good experience, seeing how different Constables worked."

"Did any of those Constables do anything that you thought be seriously against the rules?" snapped Sharp.

Morris Murder

"No, sir. They seemed a good bunch of chaps. Of course, they took the mickey out of me being the new boy, but it was all good-natured, and I didn't mind."

"Did any of them bully you, would you say?" continued Sharp.

"No, nothing like that." By now, Jim was getting a bit flustered. Peggy leant over and tapped her hand on his arm to signal that he should try to keep cool.

"What about Constable Flowers? How did you get on with him?"

"Very well, I think," replied Jim, trying to keep his answers succinct, as Peggy had advised him beforehand. "He was the last Constable I went with before being sent to Stowmarket on my first solo beat."

Sharp peered at his notes and nodded. "He was based around Ipswich town centre on foot patrol, I see."

"Yes, it was quite busy. As soon as we dealt with one incident, another one came in."

"I would like you to cast your mind back to the last afternoon you were with him, Friday 10th January 2014. I have a copy of your pocketbook from that day that you surrendered before joining CID. It simply says. 'Attended suspected

Morris Murder

shoplifting at Dennys, Buttermarket.' What do you remember about that?"

Jim paused to collect his thoughts and took a sip of water for his mouth that seemed to have dried up. "It was at the end of the afternoon, probably about 4 pm, I think. We were due to leave off at 5 pm, and Constable Flowers said that he hoped it would not take too long. It was a small ladies' clothes shop, and the owner had stopped a customer and taken them to her office. She said she had seen the woman shove a fancy lingerie set down the front of her trousers. When we arrived, she asked her to pull the goods out, and she did. It still had the price tags on, and she admitted that she had tried to take it without paying. She was in tears and said she had never done anything like this. The stupid thing was that she had plenty of money and a credit card in her purse. She could have easily have paid for the goods. She also had her driving license in there, and I radioed the station to determine whether she had any previous offences. They said, 'No, she is not on the system.' The shopkeeper was happy to leave us to deal with it and said the woman would be banned from the shop from now on. I know a lot of shopkeepers don't want the trouble of attending court. Since we had established her name and address, Constable Flowers said we would release her for the time being and wait to see whether charges were to

Morris Murder

be made. After she had gone, he told me he would sort it out on Monday morning, and we should get back to the station and sign off shift."

"Why didn't you arrest the woman and take her back with you?" queried the Inspector.

"Flowers reckoned that the bosses had been on about too much overtime being booked. He reckoned she would probably be let off with a caution, being a first offence, but she would sweat about it over the weekend, which may be more of a deterrent."

"What happened next?"

"I don't know, really. As I said, I moved to the Stowmarket area the following Monday, so it was up to Flowers to complete the paperwork and find out what they wanted to do with her."

"Can you remember her name, DC Corcoran?" Sharp demanded.

"I can't be certain, but I think it was Saunders. It was a while ago."

"Tell me, when you were with PC Flowers, did you ever hear him make inappropriate comments about females?"

Jim paused. "Well, I suppose he may have commented if a pretty girl walked by, but not so they could hear him."

"Did you join him in this badinage?"

"No, sir."

"You expect me to believe that you did not join in? A young, unmarried policeman, wanting to fit in with his colleagues, but you never said anything yourself?"

"No, sir. I didn't criticise him, but I didn't join in."

"Not so much as a 'cor, I fancy her' or 'look at those legs.'

"No, sir."

Peggy intervened for the first time. "Inspector Sharp, I appreciate that you have to obtain the truth, but I believe repeating the same question in different ways when DC Corcoran has given a clear answer could be interpreted as harassment. I would point out that you still have not told him what he was accused of. I doubt whether an enquiry from your department would be set up to find out if policemen in Ipswich made comments about young ladies."

Sharp glared at Catchpole. "Very well. I will not ask that question again. What I will ask is, did you witness Flowers or any of the officers you served with in Ipswich make sexual advances towards suspects or witnesses?"

"Certainly not!" said Jim angrily. "I might have been a rookie, but I would have reported anything like that."

"Are you sure that you have never considered it, DC Corcoran? An unmarried young man with a lot of power over suspects – you must have been tempted, surely?"

"That is an offensive suggestion, sir. I have never done that, nor am I likely to."

"Can you really guarantee that? I would suggest that you cannot foresee how you might react if an attractive suspect offered sexual favours to avoid arrest."

Jim sat there for a moment, visibly seething. Peggy thought she might have to restrain him from hitting his inquisitor. Then, he spoke quietly and deliberately. "I challenge you to go right now to my home address. My mother should be able to let you in. Go to my bedroom and feel on top of the wardrobe. There, you will find the latest edition of Gay Times magazine. I am not attracted to women. It will be a surprise to my Mother because I have never 'come out' as the phrase goes." Then Jim lowered his head and sat back in his chair.

The Inspector looked up and smiled at Jim. "I am sorry that I had to put you through that, and I believe what you say. I can tell you now what

Morris Murder

has happened. Esme Saunders was arrested for shoplifting in a different ladies' clothes store a short while ago. The manager recognised her when she entered because she had been the shop assistant at Denny's when the original offence occurred.

She kept an eye on her and sure enough caught her stuffing some sort of lacy nightie into her top." (Catchpole thought he was looking for the word negligee, but it is not her job to help him.) The Inspector continued.

"Once again, Esme had plenty of cash on her. It seems to be a psychological need to indulge in the thrill of getting away with things.

When the police came, the manager told them that the woman had been arrested before while she was working as a shop assistant at Denny's. The police could find no record of it: she had a clean sheet. They questioned Esme, and she broke down and claimed that PC Flowers had called on her at her home and said that if she had sex with him, he would 'lose' the charges. She was reluctant, but she claimed that he partly forced her. He has been interviewed and admits that he did it and is now in a world of trouble.

What we did not know was if other officers had been involved. Flowers claimed he acted alone but could have shielded others he worked with. Your explanation seems to ring true to me, and I

Morris Murder

shall not be raiding your home anytime soon. Neither will I reveal what you have said on record outside of our investigation. Your record will show that you have been completely exonerated. I apologise for causing such distress; I think you can understand that I sometimes have an unpleasant job to do, just like you. You may go."

Jim stuttered, 'Thank you, sir', and left the room quickly, pursued by Catchpole. She caught hold of his arm. "Wait!" she commanded. "Firstly, well done. That was horrible, and you dealt with it well. Now you know what it's like from the other side of the table. Secondly, go and clean yourself up, have a coffee, get some fresh air or whatever before you return to the squad room. Thirdly, I will not repeat anything that you said in there to any of the others, but I will inform DCI Webb that you are innocent. One bit of advice, though: you might want to consider 'coming out' as gay to people you choose and can trust. I know that cannot be easy for the Police, but nor is keeping it a secret all the time. Then, one day, you might find a nice partner that makes you happy, and you can introduce them to me. If your Mum hasn't guessed in private, you may want to even share it with her before she starts trying to fix you up with a woman and begging for grandkids!"

"Thanks, Sarge. I knew you were the right person to take in with me, even if I didn't plan to say I was Gay. Thanks very much for sticking up for me in there as well. It means a lot," Jim added.

Morris Murder

Chapter 13

Monday, 13th March, 2017

Webb and Cateby stopped at the café by the Orwell Bridge on the way back for lunch. "When we get back, you start checking whether the Dransfields are connected. I must go and check in with the good Dr Deborah Wilson to see whether she has had any surprises with Archie's post-mortem," Webb said through the filter of a bacon sandwich.

Cateby looked up from his burger and grinned. "Right-o, sir!"

"Oh, and while you are at it, contact forensics and check if they have got any further with the brake pipes. Particularly, ask them if it is possible that the trace of green deposited on one of them could come from a fleece jumper. They all wore them at the garden centre."

The Senior CSO Pathologist, Dr. Deborah Wilson, looked up and smiled when Ron Webb entered her lab. She was an attractive woman, and many men would have liked a smile from her. Even in a lab coat, she exuded a certain charm. Yet it was purely friendship and mutual respect between the pair. "How's my favourite detective that eats humbugs?" she laughed.

"Very well and worried about being seen offering a young lady sweeties," responded Ron, offering

Morris Murder

her a humbug from a bag in his pocket. "Have you been working on young Archie Berry?"

"Yes, he was quite a mess: no alcohol or drugs, but a mass of broken bones and organs. One rib went through a lung, and the other through his upper aorta valve. It was the one to the heart that probably killed him, but if that hadn't happened, the lung or a brain bleed would have done it. Every sign of a full-impact frontal crash. There was a powder coating of talc on his face, hands, and clothes, which indicates that the airbag was inflated. He had tried to twist and shield his head with his arms from the photographs I saw from Traffic, but it would have been futile. I understand that the car was sabotaged, but otherwise, I would classify it as accidental death, which is presumably what the killer was hoping. I shall mail the report to you and the Coroner when it is completed. Any joy in finding out who did it?"

"Not quite, although we are working on some interesting leads. Thank you very much. I must dash. There is something urgent I must attend to," said Ron.

"No doubt I will see you again soon," said Deborah. "You never seem to have a shortage of corpses from your department."

Ron was anxious to discover what had happened to DC Jim Corcoran and nearly collided with DS Catchpole in the corridor leading to their squad room. She was returning after speaking to Jim. Seeing the anxious look on her boss's face, she said, "It's OK, sir. Corcoran is completely innocent and will be back in a minute or two. He had quite a hard time in the interview, but it is all sorted out now. Someone he worked with when training on Uniform went bad, and they were checking to see that nobody else was implicated."

"Thank goodness for that!" sighed Ron with relief. "I would have been amazed if he had done anything wrong, but it is good to hear that confirmed. I remember being impressed with him when he was in uniform at that Nilton Abbey explosion case[8], which is why I wanted him here. When he returns, keep him busy so he doesn't dwell on the experience. Tell the others not to ply him with questions, either. It is up to him whether he tells them anything or not."

"Yes sir, understood" responded Peggy.

"By the way, it shows that you have a good relationship with the team when one of them requests you to accompany them instead of the Police Federation rep. Well done!" exhorted Ron.

---

[8] Detailed in *Surreptitious Cyclist.*

"Thank you, sir, but have you ever met the Federation rep? Wisdom chases but never catches him!" Ron laughed, and they entered the office. Ron went to his office while Peggy put the kettle on for a much-needed cup of coffee. She volunteered to make drinks for everyone else, including Cateby, who had returned from Forensics. She took the opportunity to talk to the team informally about giving Jim a bit of space. She was just in time before Jim reappeared, looking recovered, if a little sheepish, and she also made one for him and Webb. Ron looked through his open doorway and saw Jim return. He came back into the squad room and went up to him. "You alright, son?"

"Yes sir, thank you," replied Corcoran.

"Good. If you have any problems, come and see me privately. Otherwise, I am pleased you have been exonerated and back on the team." He deliberately said this loud enough to be heard by the rest of the team. Peggy watched and thought it was the perfect way to deal with it. She reflected on the authority and gravitas her boss could project when he wanted.

"OK, gather around for a minute, please," Ron announced. "A lot has been happening, so let us catch up quickly. Firstly, the people who DS Catchpole, DC Cateby and I have been interviewing over the last two days. We need to review them individually ` and decide whether any need further investigation as suspects or if any can be temporarily put on the back burner as unlikely. Call out if you have found out additional information."

"DS Catchpole started the process by reviewing the people they had seen on Friday and Saturday.

"I think we had more or less eliminated Mr & Mrs Berry: they had no motive and were at home together when it happened. Bob Spurgeon, the old squire, cannot walk far, let alone crawl about under a car, so rule him out?" Ron nodded.

"The new squire, Harry Scrivener, was at the rehearsal and had reason to disapprove of Archie, but everyone seems to think he is a bit timid and ineffectual. He doesn't want anything to upset the Morris men, so I guess we can rule him out, too?" Once again, Ron nodded. "Clacky Clark clearly didn't like Archie, but he was open about it. Apart from that, there seems no clear motive."

"Yes, not a major suspect at present," confirmed Ron.

"Neville Rands, I would put as a suspect though. He was a friend of Archie's, and he took a loan from him. He volunteered the information, but was he trying to cover himself?" Peggy put a cross by his name."

Paul Hicks didn't have any motive as far as I could see, so I think we can disregard him for the time being, but then there is ex-girlfriend Amanda Delafond, one of many, according to everyone. She had reason to be affronted by Archie but has an alibi for the time. I still need to check on that with her manicurist, but let's leave her out unless her story falls down.

On Sunday I went to see the musicians first. Both ladies were former girlfriends. Julie Canning was recently cast off', so she is a possible suspect, but she seemed more regretful than angry. Elspeth Charles was a partner from at least six months ago. I think she would have acted earlier if she was going to nobble him. Bill Newson seemed very pro-Archie, but I would put a cross by Peter Mottram purely for seeming a bit odd, which is rather unfair when they are all Morris dancers!" There were a few laughs.

"Excuse me, but checking for 'previous' on all of those, the most any have got are motoring offences: speeding tickets and the like," interrupted DC Winter.

"OK, thanks, DC Winter," said Ron. "I went to see Robbo Cooper and his wife Tina on Sunday. A right double act! They were against change, and it turns out that he is an ex-Banger Racing

Morris Murder

mechanic, so he must know his way around cars. He gets a cross until we prove otherwise. Then there was Roger Causton, a teacher who suddenly moved from Shropshire. I smell something there, so he gets a cross as well. Ducky Dransfield was an odd sort of bloke and not terribly helpful. I couldn't put my finger on it, but I will keep him a suspect for the time being in the light of what DC Cateby will tell you in a minute. Finally, there was Wilky Wilkinson. He was away from rehearsal but had to work nights sometimes. He doesn't like change and thinks Archie had messed up his chances of getting together with Julie. We must also check his alibi before deciding whether he joins the list. Are there any previous convictions for that lot, DC Winter?

"Apart from a drunk and disorderly for Mr Cooper when he was much younger, nothing."

"Yes, I think I can believe that. Alright, DC Cateby, maybe you'd like to tell them where we went for a picnic today?"

"We visited Archie's workplace, the Garden Centre and interviewed all the staff that work there," said Cateby. The owner, Jimmy Allsop, seemed to like him, but two of the female staff, Nicky Everson and Simone Arnold, said he was lecherous. I managed to get some information from Simone. She reckoned that Archie's

Morris Murder

General Manager Dad pulled strings to get him a job there. From the Plants Manager Manny Fyfield, I discovered that Benny Dransfield had been sacked, causing a vacancy. That is the same surname as Ducky Dransfield. It is not a common name around here, so I will check for a connection. By the way, all the staff there have alibis for Thursday night."

"One of them with His Lordship as a witness!" chipped in Webb. "Well done to DC Cateby for extracting that information. Well, that still gives us a whole load of suspects, but at least we have narrowed it down a bit. Any news from Woolpit, DC Corcoran?"

"I'm afraid not. I don't think they have heard much about CCTV out there yet. A couple of the houses on the road to the hall had some, but they were not focused on the right place for us. I can see the cars going past, but not their numbers and neither covered the carpark. The neighbours near the hall were all watching TV, not the carpark. Sorry!"

"No need to be sorry. You have had to do some hard slog to eliminate possibilities. Any news from the lab., DC Cateby?"

"No sir, other than they do not think the green on the brake pipes is from a garment like the ones the garden centre employees wear. It is some

Morris Murder

sort of rubber, but they are still trying to narrow it down," reported Will.

"OK, I can tell you that there was no drink or drugs involved with Archie's death, and he wasn't going excessively fast. The car had been recently serviced and had an MOT with two new tyres put on it. Anything else? Anybody? Right then, your next tasks:

Cateby, follow up on the lead on whether the sacked employee was related to Dransfield. Catchpole, check out that beautician, but I'm not implying you need one!" (laughter) "Corcoran, check whether Wilkinson was working, and Winter, investigate Causton, the teacher." Just then, the office phone rang. DS Catchpole picked it up.

"Yes, sir," she said, looking over at Webb and pointing upstairs. He nodded 'yes.' "I will tell him right away, sir, thank you" confirmed Catchpole.

"A request to visit His Lordship?" Webb queried. "His Masonic mate has been talking, I bet." He made for the door and stairs. It was as he expected when he reached the room of Det Sup Alex Hardy. He sat behind a vast desk in an office treble the size of Ron's, in a crisply pressed uniform. He had his usual look of distaste when dealing with Webb or other lower-ranking officers.

123

Morris Murder

"I had a call from James Allsop. He wanted me to confirm that he saw me at one of our Lodge dinners. Yes, he was there. I understand that you visited his business?" Hardy enquired in his distinctly upper-class accent with a tone that suggested that calling on his friends was not an option he approved of.

"Yes, sir, part of the enquiry into the death of Archibald Berry. He worked there. He died on Thursday night after attending Morris practice in Woolpit. His car had been sabotaged," explained Webb.

"Practising morris dancing, eh? Well, you know what they say? 'Try everything once, except incest and Morris dancing.'[9] " Hardy laughed at his own joke, but Webb merely grimaced at his insensitivity.

"How is the investigation going?"

"We have interviewed over twenty people so far and have a couple of leads we are following up. Will that be all, sir?" Webb asked, anxious to escape.

"No, not at all!" said Hardy indignantly. "What is this that I heard about an investigator from IPCC

---

[9] Attributed to Sir Thomas Becham and others – the origin is uncertain.

here in my building this morning, interviewing one of <u>your</u> staff?"

"He was checking up with DC Corcoran about an officer he worked with briefly when he started in uniform. Corcoran was completely exonerated – he was just helping them to see if it was an isolated case or something that involved others. It was in the Stowmarket area, I believe."

"I suppose that is OK then. It never looks good to have the force investigated, but I suppose we all hate bent Coppers? Very well, thank you, Webb."

Webb left swiftly before he was tempted to say something unprofessional. By the time he had got back to the office, Corcoran had already made some phone calls and shot off out. Winter was trying to prove that he was a policeman to someone he spoke to on the phone. Catchpole was on another line, and Cateby was simultaneously peering at two linked computer screens. Ron retreated to his small office and wrote up what he needed to between toying with the idea that Archie's death was a grand conspiracy between several people. He dismissed it as the most straightforward answer was most likely correct.

Morris Murder

Chapter 14

Tuesday, 14th March, 2017

The following day, several team members wanted to update the others on what they had found out.

DC Jim Corcoran was the first to report. "I found out from Ipswich Docks that Alan Johnson left work at about 5:30 pm last Thursday, so I asked him where he truthfully was since he could have gotten back for the Morris practice. I managed to catch him before he left work yesterday. He has acquired a girlfriend in Ipswich and has gone there. I checked his statement, and he didn't actually say that he was at work. He just let it be assumed. I also called upon her and established that, surprisingly, he did prefer her company to that of a dozen sweaty men! His girlfriend said he didn't leave her home that night and went to work from there on Friday morning. So, strike one suspect, I reckon."

"I'm afraid I have another to strike off the list," added Peggy. "The beautician confirmed that she was manicuring Amanda Delafond's nails last Thursday night."

"I was chasing information on the phone about Roger Causton, the teacher, yesterday afternoon," offered Winter. "Eventually, I found out that he has got an enhanced DBS for working with schoolchildren, and references were taken up with his old school in Shropshire. His ex-wife was the head of a department there, so when they divorced, one of them had to go. He decided to start fresh in Suffolk since she had put many of their friends against him. That means there were no dirty secrets to be blackmailed with by Archie or anyone else. Strike another one!"

"They are dropping like flies!" commented Webb. "We have nothing on Cooper other than he used to be a car mechanic, but it doesn't necessarily take one of those to cut a brake pipe. Having seen them, they are easy to find and vulnerable. Likewise, we have nothing more on Rands other than he had a loan with Archie. Any good news from you, DC Cateby?"

"Yes!" exclaimed Cateby. "Through going through old Census records, Births, Marriages & Deaths, etc. I have established that Benny Dransfield was the father of Dougal 'Ducky' Dransfield. Benny never worked again after leaving Badwell Ash Garden Centre. He died a year or so later from choking on his own vomit, from the Death Certificate, which is often the way lone alcoholics perish. According to some Police records, Benny was drinking a great deal and was found drunk in the street a couple of times. He wasn't charged, just put in the cells to sober up for the night. He had passed out while

Morris Murder

drunk more than once. I checked the dates, and he was fired in August, a month or so before Archie started full-time work at the Garden Centre. Archie worked there on his holiday after leaving school and had done a Saturday job there before that. What I couldn't find out was the reason for Benny's sacking. Was it because he was already drinking too much? We don't know. If Ducky held Mr Berry senior responsible for his Dad's demise, he may have had a motive to get back at him through his son."

"I suppose Archie may not have realised the connection between Ducky and the Garden Centre. Why would he? Ducky lives in Langham, so not in Walsham le Willows where the Berry family reside," reasoned Webb aloud. "It looks as if Ducky could have motive and opportunity, but we have no evidence. OK, as our most likely suspect, find out everything you can about him between you – the works. I can tell you that he and his wife have a young baby. His wife is a member of a ladies' dance group called the Haughley Hoofers. He works as a forklift driver in Stowmarket and didn't take kindly to me interrupting his TV. We need something more than that before we can arrest and interview him. He is unlikely to come in voluntarily unless he is charged. Anything else? No, well, bring me some good news, please."

Morris Murder

Ron returned to his office a bit deflated. He hadn't left any specific tasks for himself, so he switched on his PC to look at the inevitable flood of e-mails accumulated while he was out of the office. He worked through them methodically, starting with the oldest. Some were new policies and initiatives sent from the hierarchy. He skimmed those briefly and filed them for future reference if he was ever to be so unfortunate as to need contact with them again. There were internal job advertisements aplenty. He looked at them carefully, not because he was interested in moving, but because he wanted to know who was. A vacancy generally meant that someone was moving on or up since current budgets didn't permit the creation of many new posts. It was his simple way of keeping track of what was happening in the force without relying upon the rumour grapevine.

He was nearly up to date with the backlog when he found a mail from earlier today. It was forensics. They had isolated the material that was on the brake pipe. It was a particular compound used in a specific type of safety gloves. It appeared they were some type of specialist ones, which probably ruled out the ones sold in the garden centre. Apparently, they were used for handling dangerous chemicals. He sent a group e-mail to his team, asking them to find out local stockists of 'Portwest A835 35CM

Double dipped PVC chemical resistant gauntlets.' Then he joined them in the office. "Look at your e-mails," he instructed, "Find out who stocks those gloves locally. They are for handling dangerous chemicals."

He beckoned Cateby and Catchpole to him. "Did any of the people we interviewed work in the chemical industry? It doesn't matter whether they are on our rapidly diminishing suspects list or not."

The pair thought hard but could not recall chemicals being mentioned. "Dransfield worked as a forklift driver at some company in Stowmarket. Who were they?" asked Catchpole. She went to her PC and searched for the notes while Cateby and Webb looked anxiously over her shoulder. "Here it is – Baxter & Hall."

Overhearing them, Jim Corcoran, who was sitting next to Peggy, exclaimed, "I know that place!" When I worked in Stowmarket, I had to go there once to look at a break-in. It had a huge yard full of pallets of large drums of chemicals. I know some of them were very corrosive. Some guys were changing the wheel of a truck that had driven over a spillage. It had almost dissolved the tyre in one place!"

"Excellent!" cried Webb. "You can't beat local knowledge. I bet they use the gloves. I will call them and find out. He soon found the number

Morris Murder

and spoke to the foreman. The man told him workers needed to wear anti-splash goggles, special boots and gloves if they worked near the chemicals. "So that would include your forklift driver, Dougal Dransfield, I would guess," asked Ron eagerly.

"Oh yes, he would be in trouble with me if he didn't. Health & Safety is king here! We always have boxes of gloves and goggles handy, so there is no excuse not to wear them. That would include Ducky Dransfield."

"Is he working there today?"

"Yes, he is on early shift this week."

"Please don't tell him, but we will be coming to see him."

"OK, he doesn't go to lunch until 12:30," replied the man.

Webb left instructions with his other officers, then took Catchpole and Corcoran in his car to Stowmarket. He had included Corcoran because he knew where the place was and how it was laid out. Also, he had given them the vital information and wanted him to be involved. The foreman greeted them at the entrance and called on the Tannoy for Dransfield to report to the office. "He won't suspect anything. We often call them in for new urgent orders rather than dodge around the stacks looking for them out there."

Dransfield ambled in a few minutes later, surprised to see a reception committee. "You remember me, don't you, Mr Dransfield?" said Webb. "I was the one who disturbed you watching TV. Let's go to the nick – they have a nice TV set there! I am arresting you on suspicion of killing Archie Berry. DS Catchpole!" She stepped forward and put the handcuffs on Dransfield while simultaneously cautioning him. He was propelled outside just as a marked police vehicle, ordered earlier, arrived to take him away.

When he had gone, Webb made a couple of quick telephone calls to DC Will Cateby and DC Chris Winter. He simply barked 'Go' down the phone at them. They each had search warrants and a forensics team ready and waiting to move. Then, changing tone, he addressed Catchpole and Corcoran. "Lunch is on me at the Orwell Bridge Café," said Webb.

Morris Murder

Chapter 15

Tuesday, 14th March, 2017

Dransfield wasn't as dismissive as he had been initially when he found himself facing Webb and Catchpole across the interview room table. A young Duty Solicitor sat at his side. He was cautioned again, and a recording machine started. His eyes were wide in disbelief that this could be happening to him, and he looked in vain at the lawyer beside him. He had not admitted anything to him beforehand, but they had advised him to tell the truth, whatever it was. He wasn't so sure about that. He thought about his wife and baby, oblivious of what was happening and how she would react. He gripped the plastic seat of the chair beneath him with both hands as if he couldn't be hurt if he could just cling to it.

"Did you cut the brake pipes on Archie Berry's car?" asked Ron quite directly.

"No, of course not. I don't know anything much about cars. I get the garage to do all my servicing and repairs," was the confident comeback.

"We know that Benny Dransfield was your father, and he was sacked from Bardwell Ash Garden Centre by Archie Berry's father", opened Ron,

Morris Murder

seeking to impress on Ducky how much they already knew or might know.

"Yeah, so what? It was unfair. He made a simple mistake miscounting stock and ordering too much, and they got rid of him."

"Making room for Archie Berry to take his place. Did you know that when he joined Woolpit Morris?"

"Not at first. Then we were all talking about our jobs one night, and he told me where he worked. We were in a pub after dancing outside last September. I didn't let on that my Dad had been sacked from there by his Father. I don't think he made the connection."

"What happened next?" asked Ron.

"We did a joint dancing session with the Haughley Hoofers the following week. I was standing talking to Royston about something when I noticed Archie trying to chat up my wife Ann across the room. I went over, and as I did, I heard her say, "Well, if you'd like to do that, Archie, maybe you'd better ask my husband here first!" He blustered away and left sharpish. It was just as well! He obviously hadn't realised that she was my wife."

"Why, what would you have done to Archie for chatting up Ann?" teased Ron.

Morris Murder

"I suppose I might have hit him," Dougal mumbled, lowering his head. His solicitor made signs for him to shut up, but he ignored him.

"You have a temper then, Mr Dransfield. Seeing Archie every week at practice must have been difficult, especially as he wanted things to change in Woolpit Morris."

"He was brought up posh and thought he knew best!" retorted Ducky.

"He had also taken your Dad's place. Your dad had gone downhill and died after he was pushed out to make room for him."

"You don't know nothing! Don't bring my Dad into this. I'm not answering any more of your questions!"

'It didn't take a skilled psychiatrist to figure out his trigger point,' thought Peggy. His whole posture had changed from angry and willing to argue to sullen and withdrawn. Dransfield was now sitting there with his head down, avoiding eye contact but breathing heavily. She wondered how Webb would play it now. She did not have long to wait.

"You think we know nothing, but we know quite a lot about you. When forensics have finished searching your car and house, I think we will know even more, so you might as well get your side in first," said Webb sternly.

137

"No comment!"

'Webb is trying to make him feel unsafe', thought Peggy. "He is threatening his personal space in the car and home, although we may not even find anything.'

"What do you think your wife Ann will say when she finds out you are a murderer? I wonder what she will tell your baby as it grows up? Why is her Daddy not at home anymore?"

Dransfield put his hands over his ears in an effort not to hear the tirade. "Shut up!" he screamed. "Loads of people didn't like him, so don't try and pin it on me! I'm not saying anything else." The solicitor finally intervened:

"DCI Webb, your questioning is getting to be harassing and doesn't seem related to the charges. I request we take a break to allow Mr Dransfield to calm down and recover."

"Very well, I'll give you a ten-minute break," replied Ron quite calmly, switching off the mean persona he had deliberately adopted. He leaned forward, registered the time, and paused the recording. Then Webb stood up and nodded to Catchpole to follow him out of the room. Once they were clear and out of earshot, he said, "That should give him something to worry about. Can't have the suspect think that they are ever in control, can we?" and grinned. "It is important

Morris Murder

not to ask too many questions that you don't know the answer to. That solicitor was eventually starting to do his job, but it was too late. Dransfield can't ignore or forget the things I said to him. They have already found room in his head."

"I'm glad I am on your side, sir" commented Peggy.

"Better not get into trouble then," he laughed. Just then, a uniformed constable appeared. "DCI Webb? You are wanted on the phone, sir." Ron went off to answer it, leaving Peggy to wonder what may happen next. She didn't have long to wait, as Ron was soon back and headed straight back to the interview room. "You are in for a treat", he murmured. Peggy wasn't sure whether he meant Dransfield or herself.

Dransfield was sat looking nervous beside his solicitor. He had likely told him to stick to 'no comment' in the break, but Ron was ready for that. The recorder was switched back on.

"Having had a break to reconsider your position, is there anything you would like to tell me?" said Ron quite pleasantly. "This is your chance to speak up for yourself, you know."

"No comment," came the response. Dransfield stared stonily straight ahead as he said it, not focusing on the two detectives.

"Very well. I will consult with two witnesses instead if you are not prepared to talk to me."

"Who are these witnesses, DCI Webb?" asked the solicitor. "They have not been mentioned before."

"That is because our guys have only just found them," smiled Ron. "They are a pair of specialist anti-corrosive gloves recovered from the bottom of the dustbin at Mr Dransfield's home address. My officers have checked, and none of the industrial wholesalers in the area stock them because they are too specialist. They will only supply them on special order. However, Mr Dransfield, your employers, Baxter & Hall, order them directly from the company that manufactures Portwest A835 35CM Double dipped PVC chemical-resistant gauntlets. I am guessing that you will not be able to claim that the gloves used during the sabotage of Mr Berry's car were supplied from anywhere else. Then comes the exciting bit: My officers tell me that one of them has a slight nick in the rubber, which I am pretty sure will correspond with the fragment that was found on the severed brake pipes. The second witness is a pair of blunt-nosed pliers from the toolkit found in Mr Dransfield's car. We are certain that they can be matched to the breaks in the pipes!"

The colour drained from the prisoner's face, and his hands trembled. A dozen conflicting emotions fought for attention. "His Dad killed my Dad. Well, now he can miss a loved one like I've had to for the rest of his life. I reckon that it is worse than dying yourself because that only happens once. I miss my Dad every day!" This last bit of his statement was croaked in a voice cracking with emotion. "Yes, alright, I did it!"

DCI Webb made a trip back to Walsham-le-Willows at the end of the day to tell Mr & Mrs Berry that their son's murderer had been caught and had confessed. He tried to avoid the reasons why Dransfield had done it. Why give them extra grief by telling them that the decisions taken by Mr Berry Senior a few years ago were the partial cause? They may find out at the trial or from a newspaper article, but it was up to them how closely they read all of the details. He also took them the personal effects that had been recovered: a phone, keys and wallet. They seemed a sad remnant of a life, and Mrs Berry pressed the wallet to her cheek as if it would bring her closer to her lost son. Inevitably, the local newspaper headline the next day was 'MORRIS MURDER.' How could two words encapsulate such complex events and emotions yet miss the tragedies that flowed from them?

Woolpit Morris Private Members Facebook Group

Morris Murder

Wilky: *Hey, have you heard? They have just said on BBC Radio Suffolk that Dougal Dransfield of Langham has been arrested and charged with the murder of Archie. That is our Ducky, isn't it?*

Robbo: *Yes, that is his proper name and where he lives. I can't believe that he did it, though. Maybe they were under pressure to make an arrest?*

Shirley: *That's terrible. Whether he is innocent or guilty, what is his poor wife Ann going through, with a little baby to look after as well? I know her from Haughley Hoofers. I think I will ring her and see if she needs anything.*

Joolz: *That would be a kind thing to do, Shirley.*

Clacky: *I never got on with Ducky much, so I don't know what he is capable of.*

Harry: *Be careful, everybody. A man is innocent until proven guilty in court. We should be careful what we say.*

Roger: *Do you remember that time when Archie chatted up Ann? He never realised she was Duckie's wife. He apologised, but do you think it could have started from then?*

Nev: *Yes, but that was back last September. If he was going to do something, why leave it six months? Unless Archie had carried on trying to hook up with Ann?*

Paul: *He certainly had a reputation as a bit of a player – a real ladies' man.*

Royston: *Well, I think it is wrong to gossip until we know for sure what happened.*

Harry: *Well said, Royston.*

The forensic lab backed up the admission by Dransfield over the next few days. The gloves were the same type of material as that found on the brake pipe and of the specialist type used at his workplace. The minute striation notches on the pliers' worn, blunt blades matched the pipes' perforations. Moreover, they still had traces of glycol-ether, which is the main ingredient of brake fluid on them. As Ducky had previously stated on the record, he didn't do his own motor maintenance; this was the clincher, and he subsequently admitted guilt.

With a confession and a guilty plea, the trial promised to be a short one. That would happen a few months down the line, but for now, the Serious Crime Squad were set for a celebratory after-work drink. They believed they were entitled to some self-congratulation after a job well done. Webb returned from Walsham le Willows to join them. He congratulated them and praised their work. He had also sent an e-mail to the boffins who had done the vital forensic investigations. Then he breathed a sigh of relief and hoped for at least a few days' break before the next case came in. Webb also made a mental note to himself to stock up on more humbugs on the way home. He seemed to have got through a lot in the last few days and was running out.

Peggy got onto the firearms course very quickly when somebody had to drop out at the last minute. She passed with flying colours. While she was away on that and some accumulated leave, Webb rotated tasks around the team and took both Cateby and Winter out as wingmen for him. Will Cateby secretly bought an engagement ring to take on holiday with him and Gloria. He had checked her ring size from one she had left on her dressing table. Chris Winter asked his girlfriend Julie what she thought about him studying for his Sergeants exam over the next year. She encouraged him and said, 'Go for it!' More momentously, after much trepidation, Jim Corcoran came out to his Mum as Gay. "Of course you are. Do you think I didn't know that? I love you and am proud of you, whatever you are," she said.

Detective Superintendent Alex Hardy slipped and fell down the steps of the Masonic Hall. He insisted that he wasn't drunk at the time. He was off work for four weeks with a bad back, and most officers, especially Ron, thought the place ran more smoothly.

Authors notes

Although Woolpit Morris is a fictional side, the other groups mentioned within the story are genuine. Hageneth Morris hung up their bells on 10th December 2019, so they were still active in the year in which this story was set.

I acted as Green Man for East Suffolk Morris for many years on their May Day morning welcome to the sun at Felixstowe. I was also the Wren Bearer for Old Glory Molly each Boxing Day for the Cutty Wren celebrations at Middleton, Suffolk. I have since retired from both positions. The Folk East Folk Festival at Little Glemham continues to be held annually and is the best event of its kind that I know.

Many of the place names in Suffolk are of Old English origins, from the Early Medieval period of the Anglo-Saxons. In this story, we have:

Badwell Ash was originally called Ashfield Parva. The meaning seems to be Bada's stream near a field with ash trees in it.

Elmswell (originally Elmswella) Spring, where elm trees grow.

Gt Barton (originally Bertuna) Bere = Barley, Tun = farm.

Langham comes from the phrase long homestead.

Norton from the northern farmstead.

Pakenham Pacca founded a settlement on the hill where the church now stands.

Rougham (originally Rucham) Homestead on rough ground.

Stowlangtoft (original Stou) Stou / Stow = meeting place. When the place became the property of the de Langetot family, the name was amended to Stowelantot or later Stowelangtoft.

Tostock (originally Totestoc) is from tot and stoc, meaning 'outlying farm by the lookout.'

Walsham-le-Willows is probably derived from Waeles-ham, or ham (farmstead) of the Welsh, likely relating to surviving Romano-British inhabitants. The term 'Waeles' was also generally used by Anglo-Saxons for foreigners and slaves.

Wetherden (originally Wederdena) 'Wether Valley' – wether = rams and dena = valley.

Woolpit is usually thought to refer to wolf pits, but the most likely explanation is that it came from the personal name of Ulfketel (wolf = ulf) trap =ketel)). Ulfketel Snillenger was a victorious warrior at the court of Aethelred the Unready (c.968 AD to 1016 AD).

These are all delightful places to visit, with attractive old churches and homes and an old-world charm.

Other books in the Ron Webb Mystery series.

Dog Walk Detectives A group of dog walkers finds a young man on a recreation field in Suffolk. He has been bludgeoned to death. DCI Webb and his younger cocky colleague have difficulty finding out who he is or why he was there. Piece by piece, they painstakingly search for clues about his identity, address and why someone should want to murder him. They are told that he was a reticent, quiet, and inoffensive individual, so did he find out too much about someone or something? Are the dog walkers all as innocent as they appear? We get rare glimpses of the murder investigation through their eyes and interactions. Does his ex-girlfriend or college tutor hold the key to the mystery, or has the case a more international dimension?

Conveyor Belt Corpse. The managing director of a small Felixstowe engineering company is murdered in his office. Was it one of the workers or an outsider? As DCI Ron Webb and his team investigate, it appears that members of the victim's family and his other employees may all have their separate motives and opportunities to want him dead. Secrets beneath the surface and frustrations must be exposed to solve the case. Can the team believe anyone among the half-truths and deliberate lies? Is it related to a significant American deal, or is the answer closer to home?

Surreptitious Cyclist An explosion in an otherwise quiet Suffolk town is unusual. This one was at 3 a.m. and killed a cyclist. Why was he about at that time, and was there a reason why he was not using his lights in the dark? Was he even the target or in the wrong place at the wrong time? With only an inebriated, frightened vagrant for a witness, DCI Webb and his team need to solve the mystery satisfactorily for themselves and the Special Branch. Not all country towns and their inhabitants are as innocent as they appear.

An Angry Arsonist. Arson is a nasty business. Still, with so many suspects, DCI Ron Webb and his new Detective Sergeant Peggy Catchpole have their work cut out, deciding which motive could have led to a double murder in Ipswich. Money, revenge, love and ambition may all play a part. Could it be related to a mystery from many years ago, or is it the result of criminals being recently released from prison? Have they even worked out the correct intended victims?

Murder amongst the Mounds. A young woman re-enactor has been murdered amongst the burial mounds at Sutton Hoo, the iconic Anglo-Saxon royal cemetery. DCI Ron Webb and his Suffolk-based team must discover the motive before they can unmask the killer. Her ex-boyfriend seems unpopular, but at least one member of her re-enactment group was also interested in her. Could the motive be lust or the jealousy of another woman, and is the death connected with occult beliefs?

Holistic Homicide. The Butterfly Holistic Fair, Hadleigh, Suffolk, brought together an odd collection of people, but one was a killer. DCI Ron Webb was away when the murder of the organiser was discovered, bludgeoned to death in the carpark. It is up to his protégé DS Peggy Catchpole to step up to the mark and get the investigation started. It is her first time in charge of a murder inquiry, and Ron wants to give her a chance to shine without interfering too much.

Other Books & eBooks by Pete Jennings

Pathworking (with Pete Sawyer) – Capall Bann (1993)
Northern Tradition Information Pack – Pagan Federation (1996)
Supernatural Ipswich – Gruff (1997)
Pagan Paths – Rider (2002) New 20th anniversary expanded and updated Penguin edition (2022)
The Northern Tradition – Capall Bann (2003)
Mysterious Ipswich – Gruff (2003)
Old Glory & the Cutty Wren – Gruff (2003)
Pagan Humour – Gruff (2005)
The Gothi & the Rune Stave – Gruff (2005)
Haunted Suffolk – Tempus (2006)
Tales & Tours – Gruff (2006)
Haunted Ipswich – Tempus/ History Press (2010)
Penda: Heathen King of Mercia and his Anglo-Saxon World. – Gruff (2013)
The Wild Hunt & its followers – Gruff (2013)
Blacksmith Gods, Myths, Magicians & Folklore – Moon Books- Pagan Portals (2014)
Heathen Information Pack (with others) – Pagan Federation (2014)
Confidently Confused – Gruff (2014)
Adventures in Ælphame – Gruff (2015)
Valkyries, selectors of heroes: their roles within Viking & Anglo-Saxon heathen beliefs. - Gruff (2016)
A Cacophony of Corvids: the mythology, facts, behaviour and folklore of ravens, crows, magpies and their relatives. - Gruff (2017)

Heathen Paths (2nd expanded & revised edition): Viking and Anglo-Saxon Pagan Beliefs – Gruff (2018)
The Bounds of Ælphame – Gruff (2019)
The Woodwose in Suffolk & beyond. – Gruff (2019)
Pathworking & Creative Visualisation – Gruff (2019)
Viking Warrior Cults – Gruff (2019)
When the sea turned to beer – Gruff (2020)
The Wyrd of Ælphame – Gruff (2020)
Dog Walk Detectives – Gruff (2021)
The Pagan Thinker – Gruff (2021)
Conveyor Belt Corpse – Gruff (2021)
The Surreptitious Cyclist – Gruff (2021)
An Angry Arsonist – Gruff (2022)
Murder amongst the mounds – Gruff (2023)
Holistic Homicide – Gruff (2024)
Ragnarök: Creation and Destruction within Norse Mythology. – Gruff (2024)
Morris Murder – Gruff (2024)

Pete Jennings has also contributed to the following:
Modern Pagans: an investigation of contemporary Pagan practices. (Eds. V Vale & J. Sulak.) San Francisco, USA: RE/Search (2001)
The Museum of Witchcraft: A Magical History – (Ed. Kerriann Godwin) Boscastle: Occult Art Co. (2011)
Heathen Information Pack – U.K.: Pagan Federation (2014)

The Call of the God: an anthology exploring the divine masculine within modern Paganism (Ed. Frances Billinghurst) Australia: TDM (2015)
Pagan Planet: Being, Believing & Belonging in the 21st Century. Ed. Nimue Brown. U.K.: Moon Books (2016)

Recordings
Awake (with WYSIWYG) – Homebrew (1987)
Chocks Away (with WYSIWYG) Athos (1988)
No Kidding (with Pyramid of Goats) – Gruff (1990)
Spooky Suffolk (with Ed Nicholls) Gruff (2003)
Old Glory & the Cutty Wren CD – Gruff (2003)

Films that Pete has featured in
Suffolk Ghosts – Directed by Richard Felix. Past in Pictures, 2005
Wild Hunt – Directed by Will Wright. Film Tribe, 2006
In search of Beowulf with Michael Wood. BBC4, 2009
Born of Hope – Directed by Kate Maddison – Actors at Work 2009
The Last Journey – Directed by Carl Stickley, 2018
Weird Britain - Blaze TV/ Sky History – Directed by Matthew Everett. Dragonfly Films. 2024

Diary of lectures and appearances by Pete Jennings at **www.gippeswic.org**

All paperback books are available via the Veiled Market shop at **https://veiledmarket.com/product-category/books/?filter_vendor=87**

Digital versions via **www.amazon.co.uk**

About the author, Pete Jennings.

Pete Jennings was born in Ipswich in 1953 and has had careers as a telephone engineer, sales manager and qualified social worker. He is also an accredited counsellor/psychotherapist but has retired now with his second wife and a dog to the Suffolk-Essex border.

As a Pagan of the Heathen path, Pete worked as a media officer and president of the Pagan Federation. He is recognised as an influential European Pagan figure and top conference speaker. He has written numerous books about aspects of Paganism, folklore and mythology.

Pete has a long involvement in both folk and rock music, appearing in several bands, including WYSIWYG and Pyramid of Goats, and recording several albums. His experience as a disco DJ also led to a 20-year stint presenting mainly folk programmes for independent and local BBC radio stations.

Somehow, in between all of this, he also guided ghost tours around his native Ipswich and re-enacted with Ormsgard Vikings and Ealdfaeder Anglo-Saxons. He admits to having a low threshold of boredom.

The Pete Jennings website is
www.gippeswic.org

If your interest has been whetted by the Anglo-Saxon references, Suffolk folklore and locations, have you read the 'Aelphame Trilogy' by Pete Jennings? An artist stumbles upon a community of Anglo-Saxon elves, who lead him on adventures through the Suffolk countryside. In order, the three books are:
Adventures in Aelphame, The Bounds of Aelphame and The Wyrd of Aelphame.

Alternatively, if you enjoy Suffolk-based mystery books and have read all of the Ron Webb Mysteries, Pete can heartily recommend the delightful 'Utterly' series written by Pauline Manders, set around the Stowmarket area. See https://paulinemanders.com/